Vikram Kapur is the author of two other novels, *Time Is a Fire* and *The Wages of Life*, as well as the editor of an anthology of short fiction and nonfiction on the anti-Sikh riots of 1984 called 1984 in *Memory and Imagination*. His work has been published widely in India and abroad. His short stories have been shortlisted for major international prizes including, among others, the Commonwealth Short Story Prize, as well as being broadcast over the radio. He has received a number of international writing fellowships. He is currently an associate professor of English at Shiv Nadar University. His website is www.vikramkapur.com

The
Assassinations

A Novel of 1984

VIKRAM KAPUR

SPEAKING
TIGER

SPEAKING TIGER PUBLISHING PVT. LTD
4381/4, Ansari Road, Daryaganj
New Delhi 110002

First published by Speaking Tiger in paperback 2017

ISBN: 978-93-86702-36-4
eISBN: 978-93-86702-34-0

10 9 8 7 6 5 4 3 2 1

The moral right of the author has been asserted.

Typeset in Palatino Linotype by SŪRYA, New Delhi
Printed at Sanat Printers, Kundli

This is a work of fiction. Names, characters, places and incidents
either are the product of the author's imagination or are used
fictitiously, and any resemblance to actual persons, living
or dead, events or locales is entirely coincidental.

In the memory of my greatest hero,
my big brother Vijay

Contents

Delhi, 31st October, 1984

Savitri was in a state. A flush, red enough to be mistaken for blood, had broken out on her cheeks. Her bun was coming undone to leave errant strands of hair hanging. Sweat trickled down her face, playing havoc with her make-up. Her agitated feet propelled her all over her three-bedroom home, tucked away in a narrow street close to the Defence Colony market. Her voice kept pace in a non-stop rant that got shriller by the minute.

That morning, she could have been an irate general bellowing out the call to arms while wondering why no one else appreciated the gravity of the situation. As far as she was concerned, it couldn't be graver. Her daughter, Deepa, was to get married in six weeks and nothing had been done. Not even the venue for the wedding had been decided. What was more, no one except her seemed the least bit concerned. She could understand her son Rakesh's nonchalance; he was only sixteen, after all. But her husband! Earlier that morning, when she had told Jaswant how concerned she was at the breakfast table, he had merely twisted his face and asked, 'What's the big hurry?'

Then today of all days, when she and Deepa

were supposed to go shopping for the wedding, the usually reliable maid had come in late. What was more, Deepa, instead of getting ready to go shopping with her, had spent close to an hour on the phone with Prem. Savitri could have torn her hair out. The girl had a lifetime of conversing with Prem to look forward to. Right now, she should be concentrating on getting married to him. Surely she hadn't forgotten that if she missed the wedding date in December there wasn't an auspicious day until the middle of March!

An incessant rant against her family's misplaced sense of priorities flowing from her mouth, she rushed from one part of the house to another. One moment she was hurrying up the maid. The next, she was exhorting Deepa to get ready. Between the two, she fretted about the sangeet and the lehenga and the multitude of gifts to be bought. The last thing she could have wished for in her state was a phone call. But the phone did ring and continued ringing, belying her hope that it would shut up if she ignored it long enough. Muttering under her breath, she picked it up and said, 'Hello,' in a voice as gruff and unwelcoming as she could make it.

'Savitri.'

It was Jaswant. What did he want now? He'd had ample opportunity to talk to her at the breakfast table. *Then* he'd been more interested in the newspaper!

'*Ki gal hai, Jaswant, main hune…*'

'*Savitri.*'

She knew that voice and the sigh that preceded it. He had bad news to deliver. Her mouth went dry as her chest constricted.

'The PM has been shot,' he told her.

Before

In 1984, houses still outnumbered flats in Defence Colony. A decade had to pass before they would begin to disappear. Delhi would become crammed with apartment buildings, the individual flats piled upon each other in a mad rush to create living space for an exploding population. By the turn of the century, Savitri's home would resemble a pygmy surrounded by a race of giants; a single-storey Lilliputian, alone in a legion of four-storey Brobdingnags.

In January 1984, however, it had plenty of company. It stood behind an ageing peepal tree, in the middle of a street full of single-storey homes. Its outer perimeter was patrolled by a thick hedge that drooped over the squat brown boundary wall like a soup-bowl haircut over a forehead. The boundary wall ended next to a freshly painted wrought-iron gate that would grate open to reveal a narrow driveway running straight to the garage. The main entrance was actually a side door located halfway up the driveway. A small rectangular garden nestled between the hedge and the front porch. Savitri's ministrations had ensured it was lush with grass and the flower beds, bordering it on three sides, resplendent with pansies, dahlias and chrysanthemums. On sunny winter afternoons she would drag the deck chair from the porch out on to the grass to luxuriate in the fruit of her labours.

That Sunday, it did not look like she'd have the opportunity. It was one of those January mornings when Delhi becomes so cold that you don't want to get out of bed. A woolly fog was hovering outside the bedroom windows, making it impossible to see very far. The gaggle of birds that would normally be holding court in the peepal tree was huddled on a branch with their voices frozen in their throats. The presswallah, who should have been setting up his iron and board under the ashoka tree at the far end of the street, was nowhere to be seen. Early-morning walkers and joggers were absent from the street outside. There wasn't even the sound of a passing car.

Rakesh was fast asleep in his room towards the front of the house. Deepa, loath to come out from under her quilt and blankets, lazed in her bed in the room next to his. Savitri and Jaswant, who'd normally be up by this time and discussing the contents of the Sunday edition of *The Times of India* over cups of chai, were also in bed. That morning, the drawing room had been cold enough to freeze them to the bone. They had hurried back to their bedroom with their chai and newspaper, to spend the morning swaddled in blankets.

Savitri was sitting up in bed with the newspaper open on the matrimonial page in front of her. She was poring over the prospective grooms with the rapt attention of a biologist examining a sample under a microscope. With an impatient hand she pushed back her long hair which insisted on getting in the way. Her arching forehead was lined in concentration as her large brown eyes travelled from the description of one would-be groom to another, her estimation of their worth apparent in emphatic nods or equally vigorous shakes of her head. Finally, she looked up from the newspaper. Showing the matrimonial page to Jaswant, she remarked, 'That's how young people are getting married these days.'

A frown broke out on Jaswant's forehead as he took the newspaper from Savitri. He was a tall, slim man of fifty, with thinning salt-and-pepper hair. That morning, he was cold enough under the blankets to don a red, hand-knitted sweater over his white kurta-pyjama. A pointed nose, long enough to stretch over his mouth like the peak of a cap, dominated his thin face. Maybe because the nose was so long, his eyes appeared too small for his face; they practically disappeared below the bushy eyebrows looping above them. Those eyes now scrutinized the matrimonial page. As he went over its contents, the frown on his forehead deepened. 'This looks like shopping for a match in the classifieds,' he said finally.

Savitri's eyes widened. '*Hai rubba, tussi ki gal karde ho,*' she said, 'you know the Khanna girl got married this way. So did the Kapoor boy.'

Jaswant didn't say anything. Savitri snuggled closer to him and ran her fingers through his hair. 'Dekho ji, there is no harm in testing out the waters for our Deepa,' she said.

He turned a concerned face at her, 'Don't you think Deepa is too young? She hasn't even finished her BA.'

'Too young? She'll be twenty-one in June. That's how old I was when we got married.' Her voice softened as her hand continued to stroke his hair, 'What is the harm in giving a matrimonial, hahn? It'll give us a good idea of what is out there. Of course, if *you* know of a suitable boy...' she said, knowing fully well that he did not.

Jaswant's brow knitted as he considered what she was suggesting. 'I guess it can do no harm,' he said finally. His voice indicated he was still unsure whether it was the right thing to do.

Savitri was already composing the matrimonial in her head.

The decision not to tell Deepa about the matrimonial was one that they took together. There was no point alarming the girl, Savitri said. Right now, Deepa was happy with her college and friends. The mere mention of marriage would turn her life upside down. It made sense to wait until they received a suitable response. Jaswant agreed. A bureaucrat with the home ministry, he was a firm believer in giving out information on a need-to-know basis.

Two Sundays later, the matrimonial was due to appear in *The Times of India*. Savitri could barely sleep the night before. Tossing about in bed, she kept Jaswant up for most of the night. In the morning, she hauled herself out of bed earlier than usual and went to check on the newspaper, which hadn't arrived. When Jaswant came for his morning chai, he found her pacing the drawing room in her nightgown. He told her to sit down, the newspaper would come in its own sweet time. It wasn't long, though, before she was once again up on her feet and out on the front porch. Jaswant, realizing he couldn't possibly get her to stay still, concentrated on his tea.

When *The Times of India* finally sailed into the front porch, Savitri ran to collect it. She began flipping the pages over the instant she stepped back inside the glass sliding doors. Deepa, who was up by now, and had come to have chai with her parents, watched her with a bemused face.

'What're you looking for, Mummy?' she asked.

'Your matrimonial, dear,' Savitri replied without thinking.

'WHAT?'

The word rocketed out of Deepa with a force that knocked Savitri back a step. Deepa's almond eyes were incredulous. Her long face, framed by straight, black hair on both sides, was drawn in an expression that screamed, *What the hell!*

Savitri stole a glance at Jaswant before saying, 'Don't worry, beta. No one is going to force you into anything. You will have a say in whatever happens.'

She looked at Jaswant who nodded. Deepa continued to stare at her. 'You never even told me,' she said.

'We were going to when the time came, beta,' Savitri said.

She put her arm round Deepa's shoulders. Deepa shrugged it off. 'That's not the way I want to get married, Mummy. In fact, I don't even *want* to get married right now.'

'That's no way to talk to your mother,' Jaswant said.

'But, Daddy, you and Mummy should understand…'

'Deepa, when a girl gets old enough it is the responsibility of her parents to marry her off. You'll soon be twenty-one.'

'BUT I DON'T WANT TO GET MARRIED.'

Jaswant's nose pointed at Deepa like a dagger. His lips were clenched together. Savitri could sense he was close to exploding. The last thing she wanted was a shouting match between the two of them. Not with the maidservant due any minute.

'Deepa, go to my room, we'll talk there,' she intervened. Turning to Jaswant, she added, 'Let me talk to her.'

Deepa remained where she was.

'Come on, Deepa, let's go to my room,' Savitri said.

This time there was an edge in her voice. For an instant, it appeared that Deepa would ignore her. Then she swung around to flounce in the direction of the master bedroom. Savitri, with a glance at Jaswant that told him to stay calm, she had the matter in hand, followed her.

In the bedroom, she settled next to Deepa on the unmade bed.

'We are your parents, Deepa,' she said. 'We only want what's best for you.'

'But I don't want to get married.'

'Why don't we just wait and see what the

response to the ad is? Who knows, there might actually be a boy you like?'

'Oh, Mummy, why can't you understand? I don't want to get married, I don't want to get married, I don't want to get married.'

She burst into tears. Savitri was taken aback. It was understandable for a girl of Deepa's age to be somewhat upset at the prospect of marriage. It meant leaving her home and family to start a whole new life. But this...

Then a thought struck her. 'You're not involved with someone?' she asked.

Deepa stopped crying. Swallowing, she gazed at Savitri. The blood drained from Savitri's face. Her worst nightmare had just come true.

His name was Prem Kohli. He was a second-year MBA student at Delhi University. He was a Sikh, even though he was clean-shaven and wore his hair short.

He had entered Deepa's life a little more than a year ago. She had been alighting from the University Special in front of Hindu College, when she'd seen him standing on the pavement with his hands thrust deep in his trouser pockets. He was tall, fair and broad-shouldered, with full lips, a Roman nose and a prominent cleft distinguishing his square chin. His most arresting feature was a pair of blue eyes, a turquoise blue she had never seen before in an Indian face. Normally, she would have averted her eyes from him and gone on her way, but those blue eyes had made her stop and stare. By the time she'd snapped out of the stare, several seconds had passed. She'd hurried away from the spot, an embarrassed flush breaking out on her cheeks. God, how could she have been so brazen?

She saw him again in her college canteen, then in the garden outside her classroom, then at the bus stop where she caught the University Special that took her home... He was always in the company of a gangly boy with long, curly hair. Not a day went by when she did not run across him at least once. She became familiar with the red pullover he preferred, the brown windcheater he wore on especially cold days, his invariably well-polished black leather shoes, the wave in his hair that grew less pronounced when he did not shampoo...

After he had become aware of Deepa's eyes on him, he would try to catch her staring at him again. She would always look away in confused embarrassment when he caught her eye. When he thought she wasn't looking, his eyes would rake her from head to toe. Heat rose in her cheeks when she felt them caress her neck or drift slowly over her breasts. When she was alone, she'd catch herself thinking of the way they would move over her, like a lover's hands, and feel herself grow warm.

She finally met him at a birthday party in Greater Kailash. She had gone there with a friend who knew the birthday girl, a final-year student at Miranda House. That night, the air was nippy rather than cold, the kind of chill that prods the skin rather than stabbing all the way through it to the bone. Many guests were outside in the garden, conversing under a bright moon sailing in a sky dotted with stars. Inside the house, the centre of the drawing room had been converted into a dance floor by pushing all the furniture against the walls.

Most of the lights had been switched off to give the place the ambience of a disco. The music bursting out of the stereo system left little scope for sustained conversation. Two couples were hoofing it in the middle of the floor while everyone else lounged about, sipping beer or soft drinks.

She was sitting in a cane sofa with her friend when he came over from the other side of the room and asked her somewhat hesitantly for a dance. She rose to her feet immediately.

Normally, she was far too conscious of cutting an ungainly figure to enjoy dancing. That night, the music hit her in a way it never had before. Ordinarily, it would swirl all round her as she tried her damnedest to catch up with its rhythm while trying not to look too awkward. That night, the melody flowed in to inhabit every inch of her body. Instead of her arms and feet chasing the music, her movement grew out of the beat throbbing in her heart. Her inhibitions evaporated and she threw herself into the dance with an abandon she did not know she possessed. Midway through the dance, he held her close, and she felt it was the most natural thing in the world. Without a second thought, she surprised him by dipping almost to the floor. It was only when she was rising out of the dip that she realized what she had done.

After the song wound down, she stood breathing hard, a little winded by her effort. He was shuffling about nervously. Surely he was going to say something. He hadn't even told her his name! She was ready to give up and go back to her friend with a muttered thanks when he said, 'I'm Prem.'

She smiled, more out of relief than anything else. 'Deepa,' she said, extending her hand.

* * *

Later, he told her that she had almost scared him off with her dancing. The way she was moving made him wonder whether he could keep up with her. She cut him off with a terse, 'You were thinking *kudi uddi hui ay*, right?' From the way his face coloured, she knew she had hit bullseye.

The party was on a Saturday. From Monday morning, he began to attach himself to her the moment she got off her University Special. 'Are you a vela?' she'd say in jest. 'You have no classes to attend, no readings to finish, no assignments to turn in?' He'd shake his head and tell her that he simply wanted to be with her. When she went to class, he parked himself under the neem tree in the garden with his gangly, long-haired friend whose name was Irfan. A Hyderabadi, he was a poet who wanted to become a Bollywood lyricist and considered classes a waste of time. She could see the two of them each time she glanced out the classroom window. Upon catching her eye, he would exhort her to come outside with an extravagant wave of the hand. She'd turn away with a smile and a shake of the head.

He was always buying her presents. Trinkets, clothes, bags...she was forced to lie when her mother raised her eyebrows and said, 'I don't think your father and I gave you this.' Unlike most college students in the eighties, he had a car. (His father was a well-known doctor.) Although he lived several kilometres away from her, in Shanti Niketan, he kept offering to drive her to college every morning. He remained unfazed by the loud 'Nahin!' she hurled in response. Her parents would kill her if they learnt she was being driven to college by a boy.

Even though she wouldn't admit it, she loved the attention he lavished on her. It made her feel special. The envy that appeared on the faces of her friends when she showed them one of his gifts was something else. She longed to be with him. The days when she could not were empty and dull. She waited for them to end.

She'd snuggle up with thoughts of Prem in bed at night to wake up brimming with anticipation about what they were going to do that day—lounging about in the gardens of Delhi University, or hanging out in the college canteen, or taking in a movie at Chanakya cinema, or sipping cold coffee in Nirula's restaurant, or idling in Nehru Park... Before him, love had existed for her in Bollywood films, in Mills and Boon novels, in the Abba songs she'd play again and again on the family stereo while gazing dreamily out the window. It just wasn't part of the world she moved and breathed in, where hardly anyone dated, and each marriage, including that of her parents, was arranged. It was something she had secretly wished for, without actually believing it could happen. That it had arrived in the shape of Prem was an unanticipated gift of which she could not get enough. She didn't dwell on the fact that he was a Sikh for a moment.

It was almost a minute before Savitri recovered sufficiently to ask, 'Who are you involved with?'

Deepa was practically cowering. Her teary face had sunk into her neck. Her arms were crossed in front of her chest. Savitri gave her no respite. The reproach in her unwavering eyes thrust into Deepa like a knife. Until now, she had looked upon her relationship with Prem as something beautiful and uplifting. The hurt in her mother's face, however, made her feel as if she had betrayed her in the worst possible way by falling in love with him.

It was several seconds before Deepa could find her voice. When she did, it barely rose above a whisper. She recounted her relationship with Prem in stops and starts, her voice trailing off as she stole a glance at Savitri as if to ask, *Is that okay?* Savitri listened without interrupting. Inwardly, she was kicking herself. Deepa had been seeing the boy for almost a year. How on earth had she been so blind for so long?

'He's really nice, Mummy, you and Daddy will love him.' Deepa finished with those words. Savitri didn't say anything. Seconds laboured past as Deepa, taut with anxiety, eyed Savitri as though she were waiting for a judge to pronounce the verdict. In the end, Savitri simply told her to go to her room and stay there until she called for her.

After Deepa was gone, Savitri dwelt on what she had heard. Deepa had been wrong to sneak about behind her back with a boy. There were no two ways about that. But all that was in the past. The moot question was what to do about it now.

She had feared that Deepa would be hung up on some artist or writer type. Those were the kinds of boys that attracted girls in college. They had in her time, anyway. That Prem was pursuing an MBA meant he was someone with a future. Then there was his doctor father, with one of the best addresses in town. Jaswant and she would be hard-pressed to find a more suitable boy themselves. That knowledge had eroded much of the anger she felt towards Deepa for betraying her trust. What was more, it was obvious that Deepa loved the boy. Her face glowed when she talked about him.

Savitri had met Jaswant only once before they got married, and that too, in the presence of her mother. She had been married for a year before she felt she knew him well enough to feel comfortable with him. She could see Deepa wouldn't have to go through something like that if she married Prem.

By the time she rose from the bed, her mind was made up. She called Jaswant in from the drawing room. He came, looking harried, and began shooting questions the moment he entered the room. She waited until he was seated beside her on the bed before telling him what she'd learnt. He behaved exactly as she expected.

'It is because of your laad-pyaar that we are seeing this day,' he told her. 'So many times I told you that these kids need discipline. But you wouldn't listen to me. Oh, no. "These are my kids. They will never do anything wrong." *Hun dekho*.'

He had jumped off the bed and started pacing. As he ranted, he wagged an accusing finger in her direction. She didn't say anything. After twenty-four years of marriage, she knew Jaswant's tempests blew over sooner rather than later. Once that happened, it was time to get down to business.

Jaswant finally slumped next to her on the bed. 'Who is this boy?' he asked.

'His name is Prem, Prem Kohli. He's a Sikh, but wears his hair short. Like Deepa he is at Delhi University, a second-year MBA student. His father is a doctor, very well-off; they live in Shanti Niketan.'

She studied his face as she spoke. When he disapproved of something, his lips would press together and he'd start frowning. When he was in favour, his eyes would light up while the ends of his mouth curled in a prelude to a smile. At the moment, he was staring straight ahead which meant he wasn't sure.

'She really loves this boy, Jaswant,' Savitri said.

'I can see it in the way she talks about him. Her face practically glows. I doubt we can find a more suitable boy ourselves.'

He continued to stare into the distance. She waited, her hands clasped together in a bid to rein in her impatience.

It was an eternity before he said, 'The boy is a Sikh.'

'Yes, but so what? My mother was a Sikh. That didn't stop my parents from being happy.'

'Your parents' times were different. Then we didn't have the situation we have in Punjab.'

She stared at him, her mouth falling open. *'Tussi ki gal kar rahe ho,'* she said. 'Surely you're not thinking about that bunch sitting in the Golden Temple? You can't believe that anything will come out of *that*. And even if it does, how can it possibly affect us? We are miles away.'

He didn't say anything. She shook her head in incredulity. 'There has never been trouble between Hindus and Sikhs, Jaswant. Why…'

'Savitri,' he interrupted with a raised hand, 'you've got Hindus fleeing Punjab because of the Sikh militants. It isn't just the Hindus that are scared of them. The police is terrified. The militants are so successful in killing policemen that no policeman is willing to take them on. They are also killing journalists, political opponents. They virtually run the government there. The PM has to do something.

She can't let it go on. Once she acts, who knows what will happen. We can't turn a blind eye to all that. This is our daughter's life we are talking about.'

'Yes, we most certainly are. And I can't see how *you* can hold it ransom to something like that. There has never been any trouble between Hindus and Sikhs.'

'Until Partition there was never any trouble between Hindus and Muslims. You grew up in Dehradun, Savitri. I am a refugee from Rawalpindi. I saw the worst of the madness. I saw friend turn against friend, neighbour killing neighbour… I saw people go so completely paagal that nothing mattered to them—not friendship, not age-old relationships, not even basic human decency. When it ended, all that was left was hatred—a blind, unthinking hatred that survives to this day.'

Savitri took a deep breath. 'That was different, Jaswant,' she said. 'Hindus and Muslims were never as close as Hindus and Sikhs. There was never any intermarriage between them. Then, Kohlis are Khatri Sikhs, from Hindu families. We are related by blood. Things can never deteriorate between us the way they did with the Muslims.'

She paused before adding, 'I wouldn't be talking to you like this if I did not feel that this boy could make Deepa happy. She really loves him.'

'Deepa is just a young girl blinded by infatuation.

What does she know about the world?' he shot
back.

'Come on, Jaswant, you are just getting
paranoid…'

And so they went back and forth. After a while,
Jaswant's protestations became less strident.
Sensing that he was wavering, Savitri piled on
Prem's advantages—MBA student, well-to-do
father, the house in Shanti Niketan…

Jaswant's face grew thoughtful and he went
back to staring straight ahead. He was definitely
reconsidering. Reiterating Prem's assets one more
time, Savitri left the room. She was confident she
had made her point. Now she would leave him
alone to make up his mind. That way, he'd believe
the decision was his.

It was next morning before Jaswant gave his consent. He was still uneasy about Prem being a Sikh. But he could not ignore what Savitri was saying. As a member of the civil service, he had respectability and a stable income, but he could see those would not be enough in the future. Already the world was changing, with money supplanting lineage, education and official position as the sole determinant of social rank. By the time his children were in the prime of their lives, the world would be completely different. He could see how well Deepa would be placed in that new world if she were married to Prem. Then, he wasn't totally insensitive to the fact she loved the boy; he was, after all, a father who wanted his daughter to be happy.

He suggested they meet the Kohlis for tea at the Delhi Gymkhana club. From Deepa he had learned that Prem's father Amarjeet was a refugee from Multan, which suggested he was nouveau riche rather than old money. Jaswant had dealt long enough with the newly rich to know they loved nothing more than to enter the stamping grounds of the old elite. The Gymkhana was the most exclusive club in town, dating from the days of the British. It was bound to impress them. Moreover, it would negate any objection anyone might have about the families not being equal in terms of wealth.

On the appointed day, he welcomed the Kohlis in the Gymkhana reception area and escorted them into the square interior of the clubhouse. There were the parents, Amarjeet and Kishneet, Prem and his sixteen-year-old sister, Seema. As he led them through the marble hallway to the alcove where his family was waiting, he pointed out the bar, the billiards room, the dining room and the ballroom floor that sprawled in the middle of the clubhouse. From the way Amarjeet and Kishneet stared, he could see that they were impressed.

Under the curious eyes of the red-coated Victorian gentleman gazing down from a horse in a painting hanging above the fireplace, the families split up into smaller groups after the initial introductions. The two mothers grouped themselves with Deepa, while the fathers conversed with Prem. The conversations were genial, with everyone trying their hardest to get along. Amarjeet and Kishneet were just as taken with the idea of a *khandaani bahu* as Jaswant and Savitri were with a well-heeled son-in-law.

Seema and Rakesh sat in silence. They had little to contribute to what was being discussed and most of it was well above their heads, anyway. Seema had brought a book into which she dived. She had trooped into the alcove bringing up the rear of the group. While the rest of her family strode forward with smiling hellos and handshakes, she had lingered with nervous feet, the perplexity of someone not quite sure of what she was supposed to do written all over her face. That was exactly how Rakesh, too, felt at the moment.

Rakesh tried listening in on the conversation for a while before giving up. Leaning back in his overstuffed chair, he sipped his soft drink, wishing the grown-ups would make up their minds quickly so that he could go home. From time to time, his eyes drifted to Seema, only to jerk away the instant she made the slightest move to engage them.

She closed her book and looked around the alcove. Her eyes kept returning to him, making him feel as if he should say something. He moistened his lips. 'Do you like Frank or Joe?' he managed.

The bemused look on her face indicated she hadn't understood.

'Frank or Joe Hardy,' he said, pointing to the Hardy Boys novel in her hand.

'Oh.' She looked at the book as if she was seeing it for the first time. Glancing in the direction of the grown-ups, she leaned forward. 'I haven't been able to read a word,' she said in a low voice.

He was surprised. She had appeared immersed in the book.

'This is so unnerving,' she said. 'I've never done

anything like this before. I brought the book along so that I could hide in it. But...'

She smiled with a shrug of the shoulders. He smiled back. The grown-ups were on their feet and there were smiles all round. It was obvious that everything had gone swimmingly.

* * *

Even after meeting the Kohlis, Jaswant's unease refused to ebb. He and Amarjeet had got along well, and he had genuinely liked Prem. But he still found it hard to swat away the concern that kept nagging him like a persistent mosquito. Often, it would eat into his sleep, forcing him to get up in the middle of the night and pace in the drawing room. Memories of Partition, when he and his family were forced to leave their ancestral home in Rawalpindi with little more than whatever they could carry in their hands, returned to unsettle him. Sometimes they were so vivid that the cries of hate-filled mobs echoed in his ears and the stench of dead bodies lying in the streets ran up his nostrils. More than anything, he dwelt on his parents. They had gone about their lives after Partition like the most desolate exiles, their faces wearing the faraway look of men and women far too consumed by past shadows to care about the present. The crushing weight of losing their lives in Rawalpindi had borne down on their days, bedevilling their nightly rest. The impossibility of forgetting had robbed them of their ability to draw fresh breath and experience life again. Looking back, he found himself wondering whether it was good that they had survived the madness. In any case, they had both died within ten years of Partition.

* * *

Jaswant's unease dissolved momentarily in the euphoria of the engagement ceremony held at the Delhi Gymkhana towards the end of March. He had never seen Deepa so radiant before, glowing in a zari-laden sari given at his and Savitri's marriage and carefully stored in muslin since then. Savitri had spent hours over her jewellery, most of it from her own family, taking it from the locker at the bank to the jewellers in Karol Bagh for polishing and setting just right. He had booked a plush cottage at the Gymkhana, and they had planned each detail, from the strings of flowers to the sherbets. Jaswant was determined that Prem's family should find no fault in the arrangements. Their relatives and friends had been impressed, and loud in their praise. The best moment came when he saw the joy shining in Deepa's eyes as she looked at Prem, sitting next to her in his dapper suit, their hands clasped together. How could something that gave her so much happiness be bad?

In the weeks that followed, though, his unease

returned stronger than ever as the news from Punjab grew worse. Bombs were going off practically every day. There were shootouts between the militants and the security forces. As the dead bodies piled up, so did the bitterness and anger. The calls for retaliatory attacks against the Sikhs grew louder as more and more Hindus were forced to flee Punjab.

He told himself that he was being paranoid. Savitri was right; the goings-on in Punjab were miles away from their lives and the madness of Partition was well in the past. Moreover, his daughter was looking happier than he had ever seen her. Still, his anxiety refused to abate.

A little more than two months after the engagement, Jaswant met his friend Pritam at the Kwality restaurant in Connaught Place for lunch. Pritam was a Sikh, but he didn't wear his hair long, or have a beard. The two of them had been friends since college. An IPS officer, Pritam had worked with the Intelligence Bureau since 1979.

After parking his car in one of the many side streets that sprang from the main road Jaswant made his way to the restaurant. The June sun pressed down on him, squeezing sweaty patches out onto his shirt. The mosquitoes buzzed in his face, causing him to curse and slap the air. With a sigh of relief, he stepped into the shade of the verandah that stretched in front of the line of shops and restaurants. The hawkers, the shoeshine boys and the pavement news-stand-wallahs had all retreated there to get away from the sun. Their shrill voices floated in the air: 'Boot polish, only two rupees…' 'Get your palm read, know your kismet, only five rupees…' 'New *India Today* just in, today's *Times of India*, *Navbharat Times*, *Punjab Kesari*…' He caught sight of the newspaper headlines as he went past.

They were all asking the same question in English, Hindi and Punjabi: *Will the Army Enter the Golden Temple?*

The nation had been pondering that since the prime minister's speech on television three days ago. Mrs Gandhi had devoted her entire address to the state of affairs in Punjab, criticizing moderate Sikh leaders for letting extremists wrest control of Sikh affairs. Shortly after the broadcast, the army was called into the state to take up position outside the Golden Temple.

He was outside the restaurant. A uniformed doorman salaamed before opening the red-padded door to let him in. He stepped inside, relishing the cold blast of the air-conditioning. For a few seconds, he was content to stand still and soak it in. Then he looked for Pritam.

The lunch had originally been scheduled for two days ago. But Pritam had called to cancel, citing an unusually heavy workload. Jaswant had agreed to put it off until the next day, only to have Pritam call and postpone it by another day. He had been expecting another cancellation that morning as well. But there he was, at a table in the far corner.

'So how's the Lilliput Sikh?' Jaswant said as they shook hands. It was an old joke dating back to their college days. At five-foot-seven, Pritam was short for a Sikh. Normally, the rib never failed to make Pritam smile. That day, he merely pursed his lips.

Jaswant noted his red eyes and sagging shoulders and the fact that his shirt was not only creased, but had a coffee stain on the front—unusual, given how meticulous Pritam was about his appearance. He hadn't been lying when he said he had a lot on his plate.

They settled in the red padded chairs, facing each other across the tablecloth. A waiter, dressed in dark trousers and a yellow tunic, handed them their menus. After he was gone, Jaswant said, 'You look half-dead.'

'It's been crazy the last few days. Even today I'm swamped. I came out because I just couldn't keep going any longer.'

If Pritam was working round the clock, it could only mean one thing. 'It has to do with the militants in the Golden Temple, doesn't it?' he said.

Pritam didn't answer.

'We work for the same government, Pritam,' Jaswant said. 'What's more, we have known each other for years. So you can be frank with me. I can guess most of it simply by looking at you. I know where you work. The army's going in, right?'

There was a short pause before Pritam said in a low voice, 'They go in tonight.'

Since Mrs Gandhi's television address, events had been moving in that direction. No sooner had the army been ordered into Punjab than the state was cut off from the rest of the world, with rail, bus and air services suspended, the telex and telephone lines cut, the border with Pakistan sealed…

'No one is thinking of the consequences,' Pritam continued. 'No army has entered the Golden Temple since Ahmad Shah Abdali blew it up in the eighteenth century. This is more than just about some secessionists. The Golden Temple is the most sacred Sikh shrine. Any attack on it will be seen as an attack on the Sikh faith. Every Sikh will be outraged, irrespective of whether he is for or against secession. I'm not even a practising Sikh. Yet I am having to wrestle with myself. I'm telling you, Jaswant, tonight Mrs Gandhi will create more extremists than the secessionists could have hoped for after years of indoctrination.'

Jaswant was quiet as he considered what Pritam had said. He couldn't argue with any of it.

'I hope you're wrong,' he said finally.

'I hope so too,' Pritam told him.

Lunch was a subdued affair. Neither man had much of an appetite. When it was over, Jaswant said goodbye to Pritam and went back to his office where he found it impossible to get on with work. In the end, he closed his files and leaned back in his chair. So far, what was going on in Punjab had made him uneasy. Now he was genuinely scared.

* * *

That night, he remained awake, replaying his conversation with Pritam in his head. Troubling memories from Partition kept appearing from nowhere. Soon after he climbed out of bed in the morning, the news on All India Radio confirmed the army raid on the Golden Temple; a raid that would become better known as Operation Bluestar. Even though he had expected it, the knowledge that it had actually taken place accentuated his sombreness.

In the office, he found the mood anything but sombre. Everyone agreed that Operation Bluestar was long overdue, the nonsense in Punjab had gone on long enough. There was exultation over how the army had given the traitors a hiding. The lone Sikh in the office was nowhere to be seen.

On his way home from work, he picked up a copy of the *Evening News*. The newspaper had devoted the entire edition to the operation. What he read confirmed his worst fears. Hundreds, if not thousands, of dead bodies were lying about all over the Golden Temple complex. They were in the courtyard, in the walkways, in the holy pool… The library, containing handwritten manuscripts going back to the Middle Ages, had been burned to the ground. Bullet holes could be seen wherever one looked.

Operation Bluestar had gone horribly wrong. The intelligence on the Golden Temple's defences was woeful. The place was much better fortified than anyone had imagined. At the office, Jaswant had heard that the militants had rocket-propelled grenade launchers capable of taking out a tank. The army had been unable to break through for most of the night. Finally, it was forced to use artillery—*artillery* in a small, congested area like the old city of Amritsar. No wonder the casualties were so high.

The sound of a cup rattling in a saucer made him look up from the newspaper and turn around. Savitri had entered the bedroom with a cup of chai for him.

'What does the paper say?' she asked.

He placed it on the side table next to the bed before taking the cup from her.

'It's all about Operation Bluestar,' he said.

'I heard about it on the radio in the afternoon,' she said, settling next to him on the bed. 'The bulletin was all about what a great success it was.'

Jaswant snorted. 'Isn't that what you'd expect them to say on All India Radio?'

'But they've killed or arrested all the militant leaders, haven't they?'

'They have, but they've also desecrated the Golden Temple in the process.'

He told her everything he had read in the *Evening News*. Savitri shuddered as she envisioned the scene described in the newspaper.

'Have you spoken to the Kohlis?' she asked.

He shook his head. 'I thought of ringing Amarjeet

all day,' he said. 'But I kept chickening out each time I picked up the phone. I could say I am sorry, and I truly am. But what good would that do? What do I know about how he feels at this moment? How can I? I'm not a Sikh.'

'But still…'

'I know, Savitri, I know. Don't worry. Before the day is out I'll talk to him. Make the gesture. I know I have to do that.'

He sipped his tea. 'It's not Amarjeet I'm worried about,' he said. 'It's Prem. Amarjeet is like me. He has made his compromise with life. By the time you reach our age, you usually do. He can be hurt, even angry. But his path is clear. He is a family-wallah. He has too much responsibility to change now. But Prem is just a boy. His life hasn't even begun. What will this do to him? I have no idea.'

'Don't worry, everything will be okay,' Savitri said.

He wished he could believe her.

Prem felt as if he was spinning about in a cesspool with no idea of where he was going. There was uproar in Parliament and demonstrations on campus. Everywhere he went, people debated Operation Bluestar. Where they stood came down to their religion. Most Hindus believed it was warranted; most Sikhs disagreed. The discussion could grow so heated that fistfights could break out.

At home, things were no less chaotic. Kishneet had reacted to the operation with an outbreak of ranting and raving against Mrs Gandhi. Before long, her anger gave way to paranoia as she imagined all kinds of terrible scenarios for her family. She harangued Amarjeet about his beard, exhorting him to shave it off. (He had discarded his turban years ago.) She had panic attacks when someone in the family was late coming home. She found it hard to sleep. When she finally managed, she was roused by nightmares. Amarjeet put her on a dose of anti-depressants and prescribed sleeping pills to help her sleep better.

But Kishneet's condition failed to improve. Her appetite waned and she began to lose weight. Her cheeks sank in. Her eyes shrank, hemmed in by dark shadows. Her face took on a stricken look. Amarjeet cut back on work to spend as much time as he could at home. His presence made little difference, as Kishneet continued to teeter on the edge of panic.

After a while, the worry began to tell on Amarjeet. Normally a patient man, he grew snappy and irritable. A frown planted itself on his forehead. The customary glass of wine before bed was replaced by a peg of whisky, which soon became two, then three. There were nights when Prem had to help him to his bedroom.

Seeing the kind of strain his parents were under, Prem decided to keep his questions to himself. He'd never had any interest in politics. If he ever picked up the newspaper, it was to scan the sports page or find out which movies were playing. The closest he had come to a political meeting was while driving through India Gate when a neta was speaking at the Boat Club. The situation in Punjab did not concern him. He had no more than a passing acquaintance with religion. He had never read the Guru Granth Sahib and would have been hard-pressed to name most of the Sikh gurus. He visited the gurudwara occasionally, more often than not for a wedding. Otherwise, he was happy to stay away. He had worn a turban only once in his life, while visiting the Golden Temple on a trip to Amritsar with his parents. He was five at the time. All he could remember of that experience was how much he wanted to get away from the place. The turban felt uncomfortable on his head as he sweated under a pressing sun. The teeming crowds were scary. Yet here he was, in a situation where religion and politics had invaded his life!

To Deepa, he gave no hint of the churning inside him. In front of her he affected a cheery demeanour, indulging her in her plans for their honeymoon which she kept revising. One day they were going to Goa, another day to Kathmandu, still another to Shimla. There were times when he allowed himself to be swept away by her enthusiasm. It was a welcome escape from the mayhem surrounding him.

There were occasions where the pretence got to him and a voice rose inside, urging him to tell her everything. He silenced it. Deepa was a Hindu and would never understand.

Until then, he had never thought of her as different.

* * *

He had completed his MBA by now and was working as a management trainee with the Oberoi hotel chain. As part of his training, he waited tables in the coffee shop. He did the six a.m. to two p.m. shift, after which he drove to Deepa's house, which was close to the hotel. He spent the afternoon with her. Given Kishneet's state of mind, he made sure he was home well before dark.

One day his car broke down and had to be sent to the garage for repairs. He was able to catch a ride with a co-worker in the morning. In the afternoon, he thought he'd take an autorickshaw to Deepa's house. As it turned out, he found himself hailing autorickshaws in vain in the harsh afternoon sun. No one was willing to go.

At long last, an auto-wallah said yes, but wanted twenty rupees.

'*Twenty rupees*?' Prem repeated.

'Hahnji, twenty-five should you want to go inside the colony.'

'Twenty-five? Are you paagal? It's not even ten rupees from here.'

'That's why you have found no one willing to go for the last fifteen minutes. It's too near to make any money. And if you go inside the colony, you don't find another passenger until you get back on the main road.'

'I'm not giving you more than ten rupees. If I took a DTC bus it won't even be a rupee.'

'Then why don't you take a DTC bus?'

The autorickshaw wheezed forward with a loud fart. Prem spat a mouthful of abuse at its retreating back.

Normally, he avoided buses. They were far too

crowded for his liking. But he was so mad at the autowallah that he made up his mind to take a bus.

When it arrived, he was glad to find it only half-full. He sank gratefully into a thinly padded seat in the front, next to a Sikh man wearing a blue turban.

The Sikh got off at the next stop. Prem slid over to sit by the window. A young man dropped into the seat beside him. He had been sitting on the other side of the aisle, right behind the driver. Evidently, he knew the driver, a thickset man with a swarthy face. The two of them had been conversing. The change in seating made it easier for them to talk.

From the dialect the two men were using, Prem concluded they were from Haryana. He paid them little attention, until he realized they were discussing Operation Bluestar. Now that the Sikh had disembarked, they felt they could speak freely. Prem's clean-cut appearance had led them to conclude that he wasn't a Sikh, and there wasn't another man with a turban within earshot.

'One Operation Bluestar is not enough,' the driver was saying. 'What these Sikhs deserve is a solid pasting.'

'After the gadar they have created in Punjab they certainly need to be taught a lesson,' the other man agreed.

'Yes, they have too much bhoosa in their heads. We need to hammer some akal in there.'

The other man laughed. Suddenly, the driver swore, 'Bhenchod!'

'What happened?' the other man asked.

'Look.'

Prem followed the driver's pointing finger to see a lone Sikh with a saffron turban at the approaching bus stop. The Sikh high priests had ordered all Sikh men to don turbans in that colour to protest Operation Bluestar.

The bus had slowed down to a crawl. Just as the Sikh was about to get on, the driver jammed his foot down hard on the accelerator and the bus surged forward. The Sikh fell headlong onto the road. The driver roared with laughter. His friend chuckled. Prem was livid. The Sikh was an elderly man and would surely have been hurt by the fall.

'Why did you do that?' he demanded.

The driver, who was still laughing, said, 'What is it to you?'

'Can't you see he's an old man? He could be badly hurt.'

'Well, that'll teach him a lesson then. I have no sympathy for traitors.'

He had stopped laughing and was looking at Prem. His face was unrepentant, the insolent eyes goading Prem to do what he wished. Prem's anger swelled and, for a moment, it appeared as if it might spill over. Then he gritted his teeth and looked away. He got off at the next stop. The driver fired a parting shot at his back, 'I can't see how some people can sympathize with traitors.' Prem's fists clenched but he did not turn around.

He no longer had the heart to go see Deepa. He called her from a pay phone and said he did not feel well and was going home. He meandered aimlessly for the rest of the afternoon, unable to get what had happened in the bus out of his thoughts. When he finally reached home, he retreated to his room to spend the evening alone.

The next morning, he paused as he started to shave. All these years he hadn't thought twice about not having a beard or forsaking the turban. After yesterday, their absence made him feel like a fake.

He washed the lather off his face and threw his razor into the dustbin.

Among the men streaming into Delhi's gurudwaras in the summer of 1984, a few were exceptional: they were not answering the call of faith, even though they were extremely religious; they had no questions to be answered or doubts to be resolved. Their world had not been thrown awry by Operation Bluestar and its aftermath. They were there to recruit new militants.

These men worked quietly, going to great lengths to make themselves as nondescript as possible; they dressed plainly, prayed silently, spoke sparingly. Not once did they voice an opinion. Instead, they saved their faculties for listening, observing, analyzing, while keeping an eye and ear out for police informers. They often spent weeks sizing up potential recruits; they were aware the gurudwaras were crawling with plainclothes policemen looking to penetrate militant organizations. Many had their subjects followed to make sure they were not planted by the police before making contact.

One of these men was a lanky, grave-looking ex-subedar-major from the army. In the gurudwara that Prem began to frequent the day after the incident in the bus, he wore a shirt and trousers and a plain red turban. In another gurudwara in old Delhi, he donned a kurta-pyjama, coloured his beard with henna, and tied a yellow turban in tiers. In still another gurudwara, he wore glasses, dyed his beard white and put on the white turban of a Namdhari Sikh. He changed his name each time he changed gurudwaras. In the gurudwara Prem visited, he was called Surjit.

* * *

Surjit had Prem followed before he met with him. He usually had his subjects shadowed for a week to make sure they were not undercover policemen. In Prem's case, it was more than two weeks before he was satisfied. He singled him out for special attention, because of his background. Most militants were uneducated farm-boys or lower-class migrants to the city. Prem, on the other hand, was an educated city boy with a well-to-do father. He came from a class of Sikhs that had prospered under the government. He could very well have been planted by the police.

Surjit understood that the anger sweeping the Sikh community after Operation Bluestar presented a rare opportunity to bring the militancy to the nation's capital. In order to accomplish that, the movement needed Delhi's Sikhs; outsiders from rural Punjab could only do so much. To that end, someone like Prem was a godsend. His education and social position made him officer material in military parlance—which was exactly what the movement needed. It had enough foot soldiers. Surjit was willing to do what he could to recruit him.

One evening, he followed Prem from the gurudwara on his scooter. He didn't want to talk to him in the gurudwara; it was far too risky with all the undercover policemen around. For almost twenty minutes he tailed him, making sure there was at least one vehicle between him and Prem's white Maruti. Near Chanakya cinema, Prem swung off the main road to go into Nirula's restaurant. After some hesitation, Surjit followed him in.

In a decade, a booming economy would make people like Surjit, from India's lower middle classes, commonplace in a fast-food restaurant like Nirula's. In 1984, however, the place was above his station, which was why he entered it with trepidation. Once inside, he found much of the menu incomprehensible and the rock'n'roll music overhead disconcerting. But he stayed, realizing this was as good an opportunity as any to talk to Prem.

He ordered coffee in halting English. After collecting his cup, he stood about waiting. It was six-thirty. The restaurant was packed with people who had just seen the matinee show at the neighbouring cinema. Surjit stood about until all the tables were taken. Then he weaved his way through the crowds of people to Prem's table.

'Please, sirji, I may sit here?' he asked, pointing to the empty chair across the table from Prem.

Prem looked up from his food. He wasn't keen on company. A quick glance round the restaurant informed him that all the other tables were occupied.

'Please, sirji,' Surjit persisted.

Prem shrugged his shoulders and motioned for him to sit. Surjit thanked him and settled in the chair in front of him.

'If I may, sirji, I have seen you in the gurudwara,' Surjit said.

Prem, who was about to resume eating, paused in the act of picking up his french fries.

'You go there a lot. It's good to see such piety in a young man like you,' Surjit said.

He had switched over to Punjabi. His initial disquiet at being in a place like Nirula's had disappeared.

'These are such tough times for our people,' he said with a grim face. 'The things the army did in the Golden Temple—burning down the library, killing innocents, what they are doing even now in Punjab.' He shook his head. 'And to think we Sikhs have given our lifeblood to this country. I spent thirty years in the army. *Thirty years*. Twice I was shot in encounters with the Pakistanis. I have shrapnel in my arm, in my leg. And what did I get in return? The dead body of my only son, my Gurmeet, just eighteen years old, shot dead by the Punjab Police on suspicion of being a militant… I went to the courts. I spoke to government officials and ministers. I went to the newspapers… I asked everyone how can a boy whose father has put his life on the line to defend this country take up arms against it. But nobody listened to me. *Nobody.*' His voice broke as he finished. His eyes were brimming with tears.

Prem had heard countless stories in the gurudwara relating experiences similar to Surjit's, but this account, described with such intensity, deeply affected him. A wave of sadness rose inside him. 'How did it ever come to this?' he said in a low voice.

Surjit dried his eyes with his hands. 'It is this government,' he said, 'this Hindu government. Oh, I know they have a few Muslims and Sikhs in it. But that is window dressing. The real power lies with the Hindus. And they are determined to humiliate us. They are jealous of us. We Sikhs are simply too successful. Punjab was destroyed during Partition. We have rebuilt it with our bare hands. Today it is the most prosperous state in India. Not only have we done well in India, we have done well abroad too—in Britain, in Canada, in America. That makes the Hindus nervous. They are scared one day we will rise and challenge them. So they want to crush us, beat us down so that we never raise our heads.'

He leaned forward. 'Make no mistake, bhraji, today our very survival is at stake. And if we are to survive, every one of us must stand up and be counted. I know a lot of rubbish gets talked in the gurudwara these days by people who simply want to talk. They are not interested in doing anything. But I know some people who do more than talk. Would you like to meet them?'

His intense eyes bored into Prem. A tightness gathered in Prem's chest. He knew what Surjit was talking about.

'Maybe you need some time to think about it,' Surjit said when Prem did not say anything. 'That's okay. I'll see you after a few days. *Sat sri akal.*'

He left with the Sikh greeting. It was only after he was gone that Prem realized he hadn't told him his name. Nor, for that matter, had he asked for his.

That night, Savitri could see that Jaswant had plenty on his mind. Normally, he was effusive at the dinner table. By dinnertime, he would have washed the concerns and fatigue from work out of his system and discarded his street clothes for a comfortable kurta-pyjama. He'd lean back in his chair at the head of the dining table and savour his meal while conversing with Rakesh and Deepa.

That night, he sat hunched over his food, not uttering a word. His sombre face was lined; the face of a man grappling with something that was as vexing as it was distressing. He ate as if on autopilot, his hand moving mechanically between his mouth and the plate. He was far too sequestered in his own thoughts to pay attention to what he was eating or, for that matter, to anything going on around him. Rakesh was talking excitedly about a school play in which he was participating. At one point, he even stood up to deliver a piece of dialogue. Deepa and Savitri cheered. Jaswant did not utter a word. He didn't seem to have heard anything. Seeing the disappointment on Rakesh's face, Savitri prodded Jaswant. He started. When she told him what Rakesh had done, he muttered *good*, before plunging back into whatever he had in his mind. After dinner, while the rest of the family watched *Hum Log*, the new serial being broadcast on Doordarshan, he sat still on the sofa with a preoccupied face. The only time he appeared to be in the room was when the children went up to him to say goodnight.

After Deepa and Rakesh had gone off to bed, Savitri went back into the kitchen to warm two glasses of milk for Jaswant and herself. They usually sat up talking for a while. On most days, it was the only time the two of them had to themselves, what with Jaswant's office and the children and running the house... More often than not, that was when they discussed family matters, whether it was something to do with money or the upkeep of the house or an issue concerning the children. Sometimes, their conversation simply revolved round how they had spent their day. Other times, they indulged themselves a little, reminiscing about when they were younger and more fanciful.

That night she could tell the discussion was going to be serious.

She made her way back to the drawing room with two steaming mugs. The TV was still on, and a short feature on national integration, with three boys, a Hindu, a Muslim and a Sikh, was playing. The Sikh boy was new. In the past, there had only been a Hindu boy and a Muslim boy.

'What's on your mind?' she asked, handing Jaswant his mug.

He placed it on the table in front of him and switched off the TV. Savitri settled next to him in the sofa.

'I've been thinking about Prem,' he told her. 'I can see a change coming over him.'

Savitri had noticed that as well. Last night, they had hosted the Kohlis for dinner. Prem had been far from his usual cheerful self. He had barely spoken a word all night. Then there was his stubble and long hair.

'The Sikhs are furious about Operation Bluestar,' Jaswant said, 'and the government isn't helping with its bungling. No one up there seems to realize the issue is not the militants holed up in the Golden Temple, but the destruction of the temple itself. Then there are the bigots and fanatics on both sides.'

He puckered his lips. 'I saw it happen during Partition,' he said. 'Before '47 we were all Indians. Then suddenly everything changed and we became Hindu and Muslim.'

'Things are not *that* bad,' Savitri said.

'Maybe not. Maybe I am just being paranoid. But one thing is certain. The world is not what it used to be and we have to take stock of that. This is our daughter's life we are talking about.'

Savitri reminded him that his milk was getting

cold. He sipped it absentmindedly. She reflected on what he had just said. She had to admit his concern was justified.

'I'll talk to Deepa,' she told him. 'Prem might have said something to her.'

They finished their milk in silence. After depositing the empty mugs in the kitchen sink for the maid to wash in the morning, Savitri joined Jaswant in bed. Sleep, however, was a long time coming for both of them.

* * *

In the morning, Savitri waited until the maid was gone. Then she made her way to Deepa's room. Rakesh was at school and Jaswant at work.

Like the other rooms in the house, Deepa's room had a high ceiling and blue walls. A white ceiling fan, showing its age with the occasional squeak, swirled above. A big window with red curtains looked out over the garden. The window was closed that day, with the curtains half-drawn to keep out the worst of the summer heat. Posters of pop stars and Bollywood actors were pasted on the walls. A calendar that hadn't been turned over since March dangled from a nail in front of the desk that had been pushed against the wall. The desk was bare now. During Deepa's college days, it had been a mess, with books, notebooks and papers strewn all over it. After her final-year examinations in May, Deepa had crammed all the stuff piled up on the desk into one of shelves of the steel almirah standing in one corner. What could not be fitted in the almirah was stuffed into the squat bookcase next to the bed. Deepa, dressed in a pair of jeans and a white t-shirt, was lying in bed with a book.

'*Gone with the Wind*,' Savitri read the title on the cover. 'I thought you had finished it.'

'No, I still have a hundred pages to go,' Deepa said. She closed the book and sat up in bed. When her mother came to her room like that, she usually had something to say.

Savitri smoothed out her yellow kameez before sitting down on the edge of the bed. 'I wanted to talk to you about Prem,' she said. 'Your father and I are worried. He's acting strange. Last night he didn't utter a word, just sat there in a corner all by himself. Then he's not shaving, not cutting his hair. What's going on?'

Deepa had turned away from her. Savitri slid closer and put an arm round her shoulders. 'Have the two of you talked about what happened at the Golden Temple?' she asked.

Deepa shook her head.

'You have to, beta,' Savitri said as gently as she could. 'I know you love him and he loves you. But the world is changing and what is happening is bigger than both of you. It's better to sort things out now. It'll be so much more difficult after marriage.'

Deepa's face had gone blank. It was obvious her mind had drifted elsewhere. Savitri wondered if she had even heard her. Then Deepa nodded, slowly.

After her mother left the room, Deepa found it impossible to return to her book. In the end, she put it aside and lay still in bed.

She couldn't believe how well everything had turned out after her parents had learned about her and Prem. She had expected protests and recriminations. Instead, she had got an engagement ceremony that was out of a dream. A large room in a cottage at the Delhi Gymkhana club, decked out in flowers and plush furniture. A beautiful zari sari from her mother. Several tolas of jewellery handed down from her mother's side of the family. A gold necklace that Kishneet had slipped round her neck. Prem looking his best in a suit specially stitched for him by one of the celebrated tailors in town. The two of them, sitting next to each other on a throne, soaking in the love of family and friends while contemplating a golden future together. And then the magic moment when Prem slid the diamond ring on to her finger. She had been on cloud nine.

Now, all of that seemed to belong to another life. When did things change? She couldn't really say. Maybe it was when Prem's voice on the phone lost its pitch of excitement and flattened into the banal monotone of someone fulfilling a chore. Or maybe it was when he began to find excuses not to visit her in the afternoon. Or maybe when he started to drift away from her in the midst of a conversation; one moment he was there, attentive as ever, the next a faraway look had appeared in his eyes and she could see that she had lost him.

Each day she could sense him inching further away from her. When he touched her, his hands lacked the warmth they once had. He no longer came up to her with his striking blue eyes shining in excitement because he had found a new corner in the city where they could steal a kiss. There had been a time where he couldn't stop showering her with compliments. Now, he seemed to barely notice the way she looked. He was always busy when she phoned. He promised to call back immediately, but it could be hours before she heard back from him. He had grown his hair and stubble, and started visiting the gurudwara. He was meeting people she did not know. When she asked after them, he was evasive. When she persisted in her questioning, he became angry. He was slipping away from her, acquiring a whole new life in which she did not feature.

Was it all because of Operation Bluestar? She had no idea. But she needed to find out. Her mother was right. She couldn't just sit about and wait for things to work themselves out. Prem was already drifting away from her. If she waited, he might get so far away that when she reached out for him she'd find herself grasping at nothing.

* * *

Prem came to her house after work the next afternoon—his first visit in many days. His smile reminded her of the old Prem and the many happy afternoons spent talking about marriage and planning their lives together, even as her mother sat discreetly in another room, but within earshot. She felt herself start to melt. Stop it, she told herself. Keeping her face sombre, she said she wanted to go out. He appeared surprised. The sun was hammering down outside.

'Do you know how hot it is?' he said. The front of his shirt was damp with sweat.

'I want to go out,' she repeated and began walking to the front door. He gave her a vexed look before following with a shrug of the shoulders.

'Where do you want to go?' he asked in the car.

'Nehru Park,' she said.

'Nehru Park?' he mouthed. 'Why?' The day was made for parking oneself in an air-conditioned room with a cold drink. And she wanted to go to a park!

'Why not? We used to go there all the time.'

'What are we going to do there at *this* time?'

'Talk.'

He stared at her in disbelief. 'Talk?'

'Yes, talk, remember we used to do that once?'

He rolled his eyes like he had no idea what she was talking about. 'We can go to Nirula's or some place else for that,' he said. 'We don't have to go to *Nehru Park*. Don't you see how hot it is?'

She had turned away and was looking out the window. She had made up her mind and that was that.

He shook his head as if to say, *I don't know what the hell is going on here,* and turned the car in the direction of Chanakyapuri. It took them fifteen minutes to reach the park. On the way, he kept complaining about the heat. She ignored him. When they finally reached the park, they found the parking lot empty.

'No one in their right mind would come here today,' he said. She stepped out of the car without a word. He followed her with another shake of the head.

She searched for a solitary bench under a tree. It didn't take her long to find one. Prem settled heavily next to her, mopping his sweaty face with a handkerchief. It appeared they had the entire park to themselves. There wasn't even a stray dog in sight.

'So what should we talk about?' he said.

'How about Operation Bluestar?' The animation in his face, which Deepa had been so relieved to see after such a long time, slipped away. She almost regretted her insistence on asking. But her mother was right, this was a conversation they needed to have.

He finished mopping his face. 'Why Operation Bluestar?' he said.

'You never told me how you felt about it,' she said.

His gaze had fallen. She reached for his hand. 'Talk to me, Prem,' she said. 'Please. You and I are going to start a life together. How do you think we'll do if we can't even share what we feel with each other?'

He was staring fixedly at the ground.

'Please, Prem,' she said. 'Please. Remember, I'm still the same girl you said you loved.' He turned to her. She nodded, squeezing his hand.

He started slowly, the words trickling out of him. The trickle would dry up without warning and he'd sit still gazing at nothing in particular. He appeared to be thinking out loud, as if he was trying to make sense of everything for himself. She felt herself grow impatient as his silences stretched and his sentences broke off midway. Somehow, she controlled herself. She was there to listen. She had to let him reveal himself to her at his own pace.

As he continued to speak, the silence receded. He grew less reflective. His voice evened out and grew incensed as his resentment poured out.

He told her about his mother's rants and nightmares, about his father seeking solace in drink. His fists clenched as he recounted the incident in the bus. When he came to the part where the aged Sikh fell on the road, his voice throbbed with anger. He said, if he could live the moment over, he'd let his hands do the talking. He spoke with an intensity that left her in no doubt that he was dead serious.

The extent of his rage surprised her. He appeared angry with everyone—the police, the government, society. Twice he referred to the bus driver from that day as *that damn Hindu*. Those words made her uncomfortable. Bitterness had invaded him like a cancer. Already it had captured a significant part of him. If it continued to grow unabated, it would own him completely. Then there was no telling what he would do.

She felt as if she was sitting with a stranger. The Prem she loved was a sweet-tempered man with gentle eyes full of love for her. This Prem oozed hate and anger.

He ended his monologue suddenly to sit there with slumped shoulders. He appeared spent; the outburst had taken all his energy. She had no idea what to say to him. So much of what he had related was foreign to her. In the end, she merely said that she wanted to go home. She could have stayed; it wasn't that late. In the past, he would have implored her to stay even if it was time for her to leave. That day, he simply rose to his feet. They didn't exchange a word on the drive to Defence Colony. When they drew up outside her house, she merely said goodbye and got out of the car.

Before opening the front gate, she turned around. He was still there, watching her through the open car window. They stared at each other for several seconds. Then he started the car and drove away.

* * *

The next morning, he came to see her with a bouquet of flowers. He told her he didn't know what had come over him the previous afternoon. He promised it would never happen again. He said he loved her just as much as before and what he wanted more than anything was for them to be together.

She had spent the entire night in tears, thinking the dream she'd had of sharing her life with him was over. She was gratified to hear him say that it wasn't and that everything that had happened was an aberration. She desperately wanted to believe that. In the end, she gave in to that wish, agreeing to blank out yesterday and carry on as if nothing had happened.

Later, she would wonder what had made her do that. By the same token, what had made him come to her like that with flowers? What made people agree to forget and go on as before? For no matter how hard you tried, you couldn't forget. At best, you could enter into a pact to ignore. What made people sign such pacts that asked them to close their eyes to the wedge stuck between them? Was it love? Or was it the memory of love as it had once been—effortless and unburdened by doubts and distances?

The sight of fallen leaves chasing each other in the driveway of the Oberoi made Prem grimace. Right through the morning, he had watched the empty swimming pool shimmer in an unusually hot October sun through the windows of the coffee shop. Even sunbathers as determined as the group of English tourists staying at the hotel had been scared away by the harshness of the sun. The leaves blowing in the driveway meant there was a stiff breeze to go along with the unsparing sun. A hot, suffocating breeze that should have blown itself out at least three months ago.

He hovered for a moment inside the glass double doors that led out of the Oberoi. He had changed out of his waiter's uniform into a pair of jeans, a white T-shirt and tennis shoes. In one hand, he was carrying a black bag with his uniform; in the other, the Diwali hamper the hotel was giving its employees. It looked like it would be a sweltering Diwali, unless the weather changed dramatically in the next few days.

With a resigned sigh, he stepped through the double doors. The heat pressed down on him as if it was looking to pin him to the ground. He could feel its weight on his body and face as he went down the marble steps. The searing breeze left his hair restless. At the bottom of the steps, he turned right towards the underground parking garage for his car. A black-and-yellow taxi was waiting in the driveway. It was strange to see that taxi; people frequenting five-star hotels generally preferred unmarked white taxis to the common black-and-yellow ones. On another occasion, he might have dwelt on the anomaly; that day, he was far too eager to get into the shade as soon as possible. He hurried towards the parking garage.

He was breathing hard by the time he got there. Stepping inside, he paused while patting his damp face with his handkerchief. He made his way to his car and opened the boot to deposit the bag and hamper.

'*Sat sri akal.*' He had been so intent on getting to the garage as fast as he could that he hadn't seen the taxi follow him in. He saw that it was parked just inside the entrance. Two Sikh men stood next to it. One of them, dressed in khaki clothes, was obviously the driver. It was the other man who had called out to him. A tall, thin man, wearing brown trousers, a white bush-shirt and a blue turban. Surjit.

'How are you?' Surjit said in Punjabi as he came towards Prem with his hand extended. Prem, still recovering from the shock of seeing him, answered, 'I am fine.'

He retreated a step as he spoke, stealing a quick look round the deserted garage. Surjit saw that and stopped advancing. His hand fell by his side. The genial look on his face disappeared as his eyes contemplated the hamper.

'You are celebrating Diwali,' he said.

The way he spoke made the words sound like an accusation. Several Sikhs had chosen not to observe the festival that year to protest Operation Bluestar. Prem, not sure what to say to that, remained silent.

'Have you thought over what we talked about?' Surjit asked.

His voice was perfunctory, as if he already knew what Prem's answer would be.

'I–I can't do it,' Prem said. 'You see I'm getting married. My fiancé, she is Hindu.'

He wanted to explain himself, make Surjit understand he couldn't do it because he loved Deepa. But before he could go any further, Surjit raised his hand.

'It's okay, I understand,' he said. '*Sat sri akal.*'

He went back to the cab with the driver. Soon the two of them were gone. One part of Prem was relieved. It was over, and there had been no rancour. Yet there was more than a little shame amidst the relief. As he placed the Diwali hamper in the boot, he remembered the tone of Surjit's voice and felt himself squirm.

The day after Diwali, Prem received a letter from his friend Irfan:

Hyderabad,
19 October, 1984

Dear Prem,

No, my friend, your eyes are not deceiving you. I have left Bombay and am well and truly back in Hyderabad. Actually, I have been here for the better part of two months.

What do I tell you about my Bollywood adventure? Actually, misadventure would be a more apt description. In the three months I spent in Bombay, the only thing that was constant was a firm 'no.' 'No' from everybody — producers, directors, music directors — you name it. In the last month, even the security guards outside the studios became familiar with my face and wouldn't buy my lies to get in. Finally, I got so sick of hearing 'no' that I decided to say it myself. I went back to Hyderabad and made peace with my father. He wasn't that keen to take me back. He was still angry with me for dishonouring the family name by going to an immoral place like Bombay. But my mother's pleas did the trick.

So I guess I am just another louse who gave up on

his art because he wasn't able to handle the obstacles. People who make such absurd assertions probably never spent a night on a pavement or scrounged for food on an empty pocket. If they had, they would have a completely different take on starving for art's sake. But the simple truth, my friend, is that I wish I were that lucky. For the one thing I found out in Bombay was that I was just not good enough. There were guys who had been sleeping on pavements for years who wrote far better lyrics than me.

But even when it is prudent to let go, there is the sadness that accompanies the demise of a dream. I was down in the dumps for a while. That's why I didn't write sooner.

Anyway, now on to more uplifting news. What does a failed lyricist with an MBA do? Well, one of the things he can do is to go into advertising and try to make a name for himself writing jingles for radio and television. You know: Utter-ly, butter-ly delicious, Amul. *Well, I have landed a job with New Concepts as a copywriter. They want me to start the first Monday in November, which is November 5th. I am taking a train out of Hyderabad two days after Diwali on the 26th. I will give you a call after I get into Delhi.*

I can't say how much I am looking forward to seeing you. Only a few months have passed since we were at the university, but it feels like years. And it seems, all the time I was hearing 'no', you were hearing 'yes.' 'Yes' from the Oberoi, 'yes' from Deepa's parents. Before the year is out, you will be a married man. Yaar, I am already getting a complex.

Look forward to seeing you soon. Best wishes.

Irfan

PS: I have rented a flat in Trilokpuri which is light years away from the posh Delhi you live in. But, inshallah, I will be in your part of town soon.

* * *

Prem put down the letter with a smile. Irfan, with his long shaggy hair, reminiscent of a sheepdog, albeit a painfully thin one. He had been his constant companion in his pursuit of Deepa. While Prem had pursued Deepa out of love, Irfan claimed he was doing it for his art's sake. Since he wasn't in love himself, the only way he could do some research on love was to bum about with his lovelorn friend. A poet had to know everything there was to know about love. It was the one theme that never went out of fashion.

One time, when they were both parked under the neem tree in the garden outside Deepa's classroom window, Prem had asked Irfan for a kalaam; something that he could pass off as his own to impress Deepa. Irfan simply turned a deadpan face at him and quipped, 'Janaab, you are not Sunil Dutt and I am not Kishore Kumar and this is not the set of *Padosan*.' Then he turned that same face towards the window in which they could see Deepa's profile bent over her notebook. Before Prem knew it, Irfan had launched into the first verse of *Mere samne wali khirki mein* in a voice more suitable to reading out a corporation's annual report.

The memory made Prem laugh out louder than he could remember. At the university, he had been itching to graduate and get into life. What he wouldn't give now for the carefree bonhomie of those days!

* * *

Irfan phoned him the day after he got into Delhi. Prem had that Wednesday off from work. He promised to come to Irfan's flat in the morning and do what he could to help him settle in. Deepa, who was hoping that he'd spend at least part of the day with her, wasn't happy. She complained to him over the phone on Wednesday morning, and they ended up arguing for almost an hour. By the time he was able to pacify her and get off the phone, it was ten o'clock. He left a few minutes later. Soon after leaving, he ran into a traffic jam at an intersection near the All India Institute of Medical Sciences.

The red lights had conked off and there wasn't a traffic policeman in sight. Chaos reigned, with cars, buses, autorickshaws, scooters, bicycles and motorcycles jamming the intersection in their bid to get through. There was plenty of honking, swearing, close shaves and the jarring noise of two vehicles scraping against each other. As Prem inched forward in his car, he could see people milling in front of the hospital in the distance. He wondered what had happened. Normally, you did not get a crowd outside a hospital unless a celebrity was admitted in a serious condition. An irate horn yanked him back to the situation at hand and he concentrated on finding a way through the choked traffic. By the time he made it through, he had forgotten about the crowd outside the hospital.

Trilokpuri was across the river in the eastern part of the city. It was normally an hour's drive from Prem's house. But the delay near the hospital meant it was well past eleven before Prem crossed the ITO Bridge that stretched over the sluggish waters of the Yamuna.

He encountered a crowded bazaar near Trilokpuri. He was taken aback by the noise and congestion which made the bazaars in his part of town appear tranquil in comparison. An unpaved road squeezed its way between two rows of shops huddled together. The road was chewed up on both sides by pedestrians, a mechanic's shop, the wobbly tables and chairs of a chai stall, and street vendors dealing in fruit, chaat and juice from wooden carts propped on bicycle tyres. The traffic trudged ahead in the narrow strip left vacant in the middle. The air swelled with the noise of jangling bicycles, cycle rickshaws clattering in and out of potholes, scooter horns cackling like hyenas and Hindi film songs roaring out of radios placed on shop counters. Flies were everywhere. Over some of the shops he could see flats, and children gazing out through windows covered with steel bars. Living there would be like living in the middle of pandemonium. He wondered how these people managed it.

He and his car excited plenty of attention as he edged forward with one hand on the horn. Cars rarely ventured into a bazaar like that. About halfway through, he was forced to roll up the car window to prevent the dust clouds rising from the road from choking him. Some of the dust still found a way in to smudge his clothes. He was relieved when he reached the edge of the bazaar and could turn onto the dirt track that led into Trilokpuri.

Trilokpuri was a new neighbourhood. Predominantly working class, it was made up of rows of multi-storied flats. A maze of narrow dusty alleyways ran between the various buildings. The ground was uneven and littered with potholes; the car was frequently jolted. A nauseating stink rose from the open drains and lingered in some of the alleyways. A group of neighbourhood kids, not used to seeing a car in the mohalla, ran beside it, often thumping on the roof and bonnet. The frequent potholes and the shrunken alleys forced Prem to drive slowly. It was a while before the car came to a stop in front of Irfan's building. Prem emerged from it to shoo away the children. He attempted to slap the dust out of his T-shirt and blue jeans, while gazing ruefully at the dirt smeared on the car's exterior. Then he made his way up to Irfan's flat after making sure all the doors were locked.

Irfan had changed. His perennially restless hair was now cut so short that it barely rose an inch above his skull. Maybe that was what made Prem notice, for the first time, the size of his forehead. Below the gigantic arch of the forehead, a nose that reminded Prem of a well-sharpened pencil thrust down almost to the upper lip. Dark smudges below the eyes suggested the kind of price he had paid for his foray into Bollywood, as did the new lines on his forehead. He was as thin as ever. He was dressed in a pair of faded blue jeans and a run-down white kurta that ended just above his knees.

The flat was a mess, with furniture scattered everywhere, and clothes and half-empty suitcases strewn on the floor. Prem and Irfan embraced and spoke for a few minutes before getting to work. For the next hour, they moved furniture about and put away the clothes from the floor and the suitcases into the cupboard built in the wall. Then they were ready to take a break. They dragged two plastic chairs out to the verandah and sat there, talking and sipping orange squash.

A turbaned Sikh with grease on his face and clothes ran into the alley below.

'Oye, Sohan Singhji,' Irfan called out. The man didn't look up. Without breaking stride, he disappeared down the alleyway.

'Who is he?' Prem asked.

'Sohan Singh. He owns the mechanic's shop in the bazaar.'

'You mean the one that practically sits on the road?'

'The very same. He lives on the other side of the neighbourhood. When the furniture arrived last night, he and his nephew were coming home. They helped me get it upstairs.'

They resumed their conversation, then paused as two thickset men with steel tiffin carriers appeared in the alleyway.

'I know these two,' Irfan said. 'They live in this building. One of them is actually in the flat below us.' He glanced at his watch. 'It's barely lunch time,' he said. 'Yet they are back.'

'Could be working half-day,' Prem said.

'They wouldn't take their lunches with them if they were.' Rising to his feet, he called out, 'Lambaji, Kalraji, kya hua, you are home early today?'

The two men looked at each other. 'Haven't you heard?' one of them said.

'Heard what?'

'The Sikhs have shot Indira Gandhi.'

Amarjeet's clinic was a ten-minute drive from his home, in a neighbourhood market in Vasant Vihar. It was housed in a squat brick structure behind a government ration shop. A balding compounder, who had been with Amarjeet since he opened the clinic ten years ago, unlocked it at around nine-thirty in the morning to get it cleaned. Amarjeet would arrive by ten, and begin seeing patients soon afterwards. That day, he was with his first patient of the day when Jaswant called. Jaswant came straight to the point.

'Listen, Amarjeet, we are trying to keep a lid on this, so please keep it between us. The PM has been shot.'

Amarjeet's jaw went slack. His pupils dilated and, for a second, he looked like a boxer who has taken a powerful blow. Then he gulped hard, his fingers wrapping tightly round the receiver.

'How is she?' he asked in a raspy voice.

'We don't know yet. She was rushed to AIIMS from her residence, where she was shot. But it doesn't look good. The shooters were two of her own security guards and they shot her point-blank from close range.'

Amarjeet moistened his lips which had suddenly gone dry. In a low voice he asked, 'Were they Sikhs?'

'Yes.'

Amarjeet closed his eyes.

'I think you'd better shut down the clinic and go home,' Jaswant said. 'And make sure Kishneet, Prem and Seema are home as well. There could be trouble. I can't leave here. The minister is due in ten minutes. But I am going to call Savitri and tell her to get Rakesh home from school. I'd better do it now, since she and Deepa are supposed to go shopping.'

'Yes, yes, take care.'

Amarjeet's hands were shaking as he replaced the receiver. His stomach felt tight as a drum and sweat glinted on his forehead.

After

'The PM has been shot.'

Savitri gasped. What Jaswant said next confirmed her worst fears; Mrs Gandhi's shooters were Sikhs. Jaswant was forced to cut short the conversation because the minister had arrived. He urged her to go and bring Rakesh home from school before ringing off.

Savitri remained rooted to the spot, the disconnected receiver buzzing in her hand. Suppose Mrs Gandhi died... Her stomach lurched at the thought.

'Mummy.' A concerned Deepa was gazing at her. Savitri replaced the receiver and told Deepa what had happened in a low voice. She finished by saying that she was going to get Rakesh. Deepa refused to let her go alone. After a brief argument, Savitri relented. Inwardly, she was glad. Still reeling from the news of the shooting, she was in no shape to go out alone.

Before they left, Deepa rang the Kohlis. She hoped that Prem was still at home, but Kishneet confirmed that he had left. From her tremulous voice, it was obvious that her nerves were jangling. She was trying to figure out a way to get in touch with Prem, because Irfan didn't have a phone. Deepa told her that she'd ring her the moment she got back from Rakesh's school.

It was a thirty-minute drive to Rakesh's school in the family's white Fiat. While Savitri drove, Deepa sat staring unseeingly out the window. A quivering hand covered her mouth. Savitri tried to reassure her, saying everything would be okay. Her words sounded hollow when they saw a group of men pulling off a Sikh man's turban at a bus stop. A policeman stood watching a few feet away. Some people were egging on the assailants with a chorus of *maaro saale ko, aur maaro*. Deepa turned a stricken face at Savitri. Savitri, not knowing what to say, simply squeezed her hand.

The drive to the school seemed to take an eternity. As she drove, Savitri could see that news about the shooting was spreading quickly. People were gathering at stalls and bus stops. When she stopped at red lights, she could see the shock and fear on their faces. Next to her, Deepa was growing jumpy; the incident with the Sikh at the bus stop had made her more anxious than ever about Prem. It was all Savitri could do to keep herself calm enough to focus on the job at hand.

At long last, they were at the school. Deepa jumped out of the car to fetch Rakesh. He came, bemused, wondering why his mother and sister had come to pick him up. When they told him, he started quizzing them about the shooting. Savitri said she'd tell him what she knew once they got home.

They were halfway there when Rakesh cried out, 'Mummy, look.' Three men were holding a Sikh man down on the pavement. The Sikh's hair had been cut and lay scattered around. A heavy man, dressed in a pair of jeans and a red T-shirt, had prised his mouth open with a knife. The howl erupting out of the Sikh was silenced abruptly as the man shoved a handful of his hair into his mouth. The crowd of men standing about and watching cheered.

Rakesh threw up all over his school uniform. Deepa's eyes widened as her hand leaped to her mouth. Savitri gulped back the bile filling her throat. She pressed down hard on the accelerator, wanting to get away from there as fast as she could.

Please let Prem be safe, she prayed. Please god, please.

'I'd better go home,' Prem said to Irfan.
'Be careful,' Irfan told him.

He wondered whether he should tell Prem to cut his hair, to trim his stubble, to discard the kara he was wearing on his right wrist...To get rid of anything that could possibly identify him as a Sikh. He abandoned the idea. He didn't want to risk offending Prem.

He walked Prem down to his car, where the two of them said goodbye. The news of Indira Gandhi's shooting had brought people out of their homes. The alleys were full of men and women standing about and talking. The children hovered, unsure about what was going on. Normally, the alleyways belonged to them in the afternoon. The grown-ups were either at work or taking a nap. For some reason, today they had abandoned their normal routine. Moreover, they appeared more animated than usual.

Prem inched forward through this assorted crowd, blowing the horn. Curious looks zeroed in on him, some lingering longer than others. But people moved aside to let him pass before returning to the business of gleaning more information about the shooting or passing an opinion on it.

It was almost half an hour before Prem was able to reach the dirt track that connected Trilokpuri to the main road. He was forced to slow down immediately because of the large concrete pipe that lay across it, blocking his way. Four young men, including a police constable in a khaki uniform, stood next to the pipe. The constable had a lathi in his hand, while the other three were brandishing hockey sticks.

The constable motioned for the car to stop. Unease clawed at Prem's chest and stomach. His eyes darted around, desperate for an escape route. There was none. He couldn't back off now and there was no way round the pipe stretching across the dirt track. His hand rose inadvertently to his stubble. He dropped it immediately, wishing he had shaved in the morning.

The constable was telling him to roll down his window. He had no choice except to comply. 'Hahnji?' he said, trying to keep his voice from shaking.

The constable was a man of medium height, with a fleshy face and a thick moustache turned up at both ends. The way his eyes travelled over Prem sent a chill through Prem's body.

'Isko roko, yeh saala Sikh hai,' the constable shouted suddenly.

Too late, Prem remembered the kara on his wrist. He tried to start the car. But one of the men had already pulled the car door open. There was a hand in his face, another tugging at his shirt. A hockey stick swung into the windscreen, sending shards of glass flying. Prem's hands leaped to protect his face. Pieces of glass dug into the back of his hands and forearms. He screamed.

He kicked out with his feet, as the four men hauled him out of the car. The lathi caught him in the shoulder. A hockey stick slammed into his shin. His legs collapsed from under him as he crumpled, still screaming, onto the dirt track. The four men started kicking him. He lay face down, writhing in pain. Pebbles dug into his body. Dust crowded into his eyes and nose. His cries grew muffled. He couldn't see anything. All he was aware of was an intense blinding pain. Then, abruptly, the kicking stopped. Hands grabbed him to turn him over onto his back. He opened his bruised eyes to make out a grinning face. It was the constable. 'Saala bhenchod,' the constable was saying, 'you thought we were idiots. We wouldn't know you are a Sikh, maaderchod.' His grin grew maniacal as his lathi scythed through the air. A split second before it struck, Prem screamed, his face contorting in anticipation of the pain about to race through his body.

* * *

Irfan started as someone began banging on his front door. A shrill voice cried out, 'Uncle.'

'I'm coming, I'm coming,' Irfan yelled. He stepped as quickly as he could through the mess on the floor to open his front door. It was his downstairs neighbour's teenaged son. The boy was panting hard. He had come running.

'*Kya paagal ho gaye ho*? You are beating my door down!' Irfan said.

'*Uncle, aap ka carwallah friend…*' The boy paused to catch his breath. Irfan's stomach dipped. He grabbed the boy's shoulders. '*Kya hua?*'

'I just saw four men beating him.'

'What?'

'Yes, Uncle. It was on the dirt track that leads to the main road. I…'

Irfan was already running down the stairs and out into the alleyway. The sun, crouching low on yellow blocks of flats, hit his eyes. A stinking open drain gave way to a warren of alleyways. Crashing past elbows and forearms. A volley of curses following him. His sandals scratching, slipping in the dust. His breath spilling out in gasps.

He halted, gulping down air, upon reaching the dirt track. Pain pulsed in his side. A few men were clustered in a circle. Wiping the sweat from his eyes, he pushed his way to the centre of the cluster.

'*Hai Allah!*' he said as he saw Prem lying on the ground in a bloody heap.

'Prem,' he said, kneeling down.
There was no answer.
He shook Prem by the shoulder.
There was still no answer.

It was the period after break at Seema's school. Seema and her friends had just returned to the classroom. The middle-aged maths teacher, a chunky, bespectacled woman in a yellow sari, was about to wade into the mysteries of calculus when the khaki-shirted peon from the headmistress's office entered the classroom with a message. No sooner had the teacher read it than her face grew pale. In a shaky voice she announced that the prime minister had been shot and the school would shut early. Once she had made this difficult announcement, the teacher composed herself and instructed the students to gather their belongings and quietly proceed to the assembly ground in an orderly queue. The buses had been summoned to take them home.

Normally, the students would have reacted to an unexpected chhutti as if to a gift, all the more wonderful because it was unanticipated. But that day, even the junior boys and girls, who were far too young to grasp the essence of what was going on, could sense something was amiss. The strained faces of their teachers and seniors told them that. The exodus to the assembly ground was slow, with everyone moving on leaden feet. The teachers, who'd normally be hurrying them along, were wrapped up in their own concerns. The students were allowed to walk at their own pace.

Seema had to stop to go to the bathroom on the way. By the time she reached the ground, her friends had already gathered. They were talking animatedly about what had happened. Upon seeing her, they fell silent. Other girls were looking at her, nudging their friends and pointing her out, turning in her direction... Nothing like that had happened before. It made her uncomfortable.

In later years, she'd look back at that moment and recognize it as the one when everything changed. Operation Bluestar had done little to disrupt her life, even though it had disturbed the rest of her family. That day at school, when she felt herself being marked out, transformed everything. Even though she couldn't grasp the full import of what was happening, some of it clearly seeped through into her. She didn't talk to anyone. When she finally got on the bus, she sought out a lone seat at the back and did not speak for the entire length of the journey. At her bus stop, she found Vishnu, the Hindu houseboy, waiting for her. The bus stop was a mere two-minute walk from her house and no one had come to collect her since she was a little girl. When she reached home, Kishneet and Amarjeet hugged her as if they hadn't seen her in days. All she could do was retreat to her room and collapse in bed. Even though she wasn't tired, she felt utterly drained.

The hurt would come later, as what happened at school would repeat itself frequently enough to become the normal state of affairs. What troubled her then was the unsettling feeling of something dark and sinister entering her life, leaving her unsure of things she had always taken for granted. As the day dragged forward without any news of Prem, her unease grew into an acute foreboding. A sense of doom had taken possession of the house.

Kishneet had waded into a dark pool of despair. When she wasn't sitting shrunken in the sofa and gazing at nothing in particular, she was sobbing and wailing in a voice reminiscent of a funereal chant. Amarjeet was unable to stay still. He paced about the house, ageing a little more each time Seema saw him. From time to time, he would grit his teeth while clenching and unclenching his fists. The fact that he couldn't do anything except wait was driving him crazy. Lunch was on nobody's mind, even though the food had been prepared.

They all started when the phone rang for the first time since Seema had got back home. The thought that it was Prem made them all rush to answer it. Seema got there before anyone else to snatch the receiver from its hook.

A man's voice that she did not recognize

snapped, 'You damn Sikhs, we are going to kill each and every one of you,' before hanging up.

* * *

Jaswant's meeting with the minister was followed by another meeting. By the time he got back to his cabin, it was well past lunchtime. Exhausted, he collapsed in his black revolving chair to sit hunched forward, his elbows resting on top of his polished desk, his head clutched in his hands. A dull ache was throbbing in the centre of his forehead.

There was a knock on his door. With a sigh, he sat up straight and said, 'Come in.' The door opened. It was his secretary Ramakrishnan.

'There were two calls from Mr Kohli, sir,' Ramakrishnan said.

Did this have to do with Prem? He hoped nothing had happened. He dismissed Ramakrishnan and dialled Amarjeet, who picked up on the second ring.

'Yes, I did phone,' Amarjeet said. 'It's about Prem.'

They still had no news of him, and now they were getting really worried. He had rung him in the hope that Jaswant might be able to help. Jaswant promised to get on the job immediately. He took down Irfan's address and told Amarjeet he'd ring the moment he learnt something.

'There's one more thing,' Amarjeet said. 'About

half an hour ago we got a phone call. We were all excited. We thought it was Prem. Seema was the one who answered. She doesn't know who it was. The man told her, "You damn Sikhs, we are going to kill each and every one of you," and hung up.'

Jaswant placed his hand on his forehead where the ache had become worse. 'I'm sorry, but you could get a few of those,' he told Amarjeet. 'They are meant to scare you. If someone really wanted to harm you then the last thing he'd do is call. But please don't go out of the house, and don't let Seema or Kishneet go either. And make sure the gate and front door are securely fastened at all times.'

'Why? What's happened?'

'Mrs Gandhi is dead.'

To Irfan's relief, he made out a throb in Prem's wrist that told him he was alive. '*Koi doctor hai yahan?*' he asked the men who had gathered on the dirt track. One of them said the closest they had to a doctor was a nursing orderly named Raj Kumar who lived in a ground-floor flat in a building not far away. He suggested they take Prem to him. Since Raj Kumar worked the night shift, he'd be home at the moment. He could look after Prem. Irfan reflected on what the man had said. There was no telling how long an ambulance would take, and they couldn't very well leave Prem lying there. He asked the other men to help carry him to Raj Kumar's flat.

Prem remained unconscious as they took him to the flat. He had a bump in the back of his head. His face and clothes were covered with blood. The left side of his jaw was swollen. Irfan feared it might be broken.

Raj Kumar turned out to be a short greying man in his fifties dressed in a long-sleeved white shirt, dark-blue trousers and a pair of rubber slippers. His habit of constantly poking at his horn-rimmed spectacles made him appear nervous. When he caught sight of the kara on Prem's wrist, he said, 'No, no, nahin, don't bring him here,' in a scratchy voice.

'Look how hurt he is,' Irfan shot back.

'No, not here, take him away immediately,' Raj Kumar insisted, gesticulating excitably.

'What kind of a man are you?' Irfan demanded. An abashed look washed over Raj Kumar's face. He pursed his lips. But he stood aside, allowing them to bring Prem into the flat.

The flat was sparsely furnished with a table, a few chairs, a faded second-hand sofa and an old black-and-white TV. They carried Prem to the small room in the back of the flat and laid him down on a charpoy. Raj Kumar went to call an ambulance, only to find that his phone was dead.

He was taken aback. He had been speaking on it just a few minutes before they arrived. Irfan asked if one of his neighbours had a phone. Raj Kumar shook his head. The nearest phone was in a flat in the next building. Irfan said he'd go there and make the call. In the meanwhile, Raj Kumar could examine Prem.

The phone in the adjacent building was in a flat owned by a railway clerk. He told Irfan that it had gone dead a few minutes ago. He let Irfan check to make sure. When Irfan asked him if he knew of other phones, he suggested he try a flat in a building a hundred yards away. Its owner was a friend of his who also worked in the railways. Irfan went there as fast as he could to find that phone dead as well.

By now he had been away from Raj Kumar's flat for almost fifteen minutes. He decided to return there to see how Prem was getting on. Then he would go to the nearby bazaar and use a pay phone. It was apparent that something was wrong with the telephone lines in the neighbourhood.

He began walking in the direction of Raj Kumar's flat. He hadn't gone far, before he turned into an alleyway and came face to face with a middle-aged man dressed in a khadi kurta-pyjama with a Gandhi cap on his head. He recognized him as a local Congress neta. There were several other men with him, including a police constable in full uniform. They were carrying machetes, lathis, hockey sticks and cans of kerosene oil.

'Who are you?' the neta demanded.

'I live here,' Irfan said.

'I asked *who* you are—Hindu, Muslim, Sikh?'

'Muslim.'

'The chootiya is lying,' one of the men cried out. 'He's a Sikh.'

Fear rippled through Irfan as he realized what was going on. The mob was in the neighbourhood to hunt down Sikhs. He tried to bury his concern under a nervous laugh. 'How can I be a Sikh?' he said. 'Just look at me. There is no turban, no beard...'

'Today those maaderchods are cutting their hair and shaving their beards,' the constable said. 'Just like that saala with the car. Didn't look like a Sikh at all.'

There were murmurs of agreement. Irfan, realizing who they were talking about, swallowed hard. He held up his right arm. 'See, I'm not even wearing a kara,' he said in a hoarse voice that sounded nothing like his own.

'You could have taken it off,' the neta said. 'If you can cut your hair and beard then what is a kara?'

He nodded to a hulking man in a T-shirt and trousers standing next to him. The man advanced on Irfan with a raised machete. Irfan's insides squashed against his bones. 'Wait,' he called out in the best voice he could muster.

He unbuttoned his trousers and let them fall. Dropping his underwear, he showed them his penis which was clearly circumcized.

'All right, I believe you,' the neta said. He looked at the sheet of paper in his hands. 'There should be a Sikh family in the next gali,' he said. 'Come on.'

The men set off like a pack of wild dogs. 'If this was Partition, your lund would have been chopped off today,' the constable remarked as he stepped past Irfan.

* * *

Irfan waited until they were out of sight. Then he ran to Raj Kumar's flat. Prem was in the middle of a fit. He was flailing about in the charpoy, screaming as loudly as he could. Irfan did his best to pacify him but Prem's fit didn't look like abating. Finally, he agreed to let Raj Kumar give him a sedative. He held Prem down on the charpoy while Raj Kumar prised his mouth open to place a crushed tablet upon Prem's tongue and poured water down his throat. Prem's body soon went limp and his head sank on the pillow.

'That's all we can do,' Raj Kumar said. 'He's still in shock. This way at least he can rest.'

He had bandaged Prem's head and cleaned the blood off the rest of his face and body. Prem had lost a lot of blood. But his bruises were nowhere near as bad as Raj Kumar had feared. The blows appeared to have struck flesh rather than bone. There was, however, a gash on the forehead, and another just below the ribs, that needed bandages. About the swelling in the jaw, Raj Kumar couldn't say. Only an X-ray could reveal if it was fractured.

Raj Kumar had thrown away Prem's bloody clothes and dressed him in one of his kurta-pyjamas. The kurta-pyjama was small for Prem, since he was a much taller man. But at least it was clean.

'I also took this off,' Raj Kumar said.

He held up Prem's kara. 'I saw some goondas in the gali outside,' he explained. 'I was afraid they might come here.'

Irfan recalled the sheet of paper in the Congress man's hands. 'They won't,' he said. 'They know where all the Sikhs live.'

'What do you mean?' Raj Kumar asked.

Irfan told him about his run-in with the neta and his gang. 'We must let the authorities know what's going on here,' he said after he was finished. 'There seems to be something wrong with the telephone lines. *Sab phone dead hain*. I'll have to go to the bazaar for a pay phone. I'll call for the ambulance too.'

'What kind of bakwaas are you talking?' Raj Kumar snapped. He pushed rather than poked at his spectacles as he said, 'Are you paagal?'

Irfan stared at him. 'What do you mean?' he demanded. Pointing to Prem he said, *'Iska condition dekh rahe ho*. There is a pack of wild dogs running amok in this neighbourhood. If we don't get the word out they will spread gadar.'

'If *you* go then your friend goes with you,' Raj Kumar said.

'What?'

'You got lucky once,' Raj Kumar continued. 'Your Allah was smiling on you. But what do you think will happen if these goondas catch you trying to sneak out of the neighbourhood? You say *phone dead hain. Main bataata hoon kyun*. These thugs have cut the telephone wires. They are not going to let even a makkhi out of here.'

'But I...'

'No buts. You go and your friend goes with you. They let you live last time because they thought you were not involved. But if they catch you trying to sneak out, they will not spare you. And before they kill you, they will make you tell them why you want to leave. And then they will come here. You may not care what happens to you. But I have my whole khandaan in my village. They depend on me for their lives. I can't afford to get killed.'

They started as a hail of fists rained down on Raj Kumar's front door. A voice cried out, 'Bhaisahib, jaldi, there are goondas in our flat.'

Irfan stepped towards the door. Raj Kumar grabbed his wrist. He was shaking his head. They remained where they were until the din died and they could hear the sound of running feet. Irfan slumped in a chair to gaze unseeingly in front of him. Raj Kumar settled on a stool on the other side of the room. Taking off his spectacles, he rubbed his eyes.

'This is all new for you, isn't it?' he said, after putting his spectacles back on. 'You may be here now, but you don't come from a mohalla like this one. You come from a nice part of town where such things happen only in newspapers. *Aaj ki taaza khabar*. Believe me, there is nothing you can do. I've seen this since I was a child. It's the same every time. All that changes is the face of the victim. Today it's the Sikhs. Tomorrow it will be someone else. Just thank your kismet it's not you they are after.'

The evening sky had deadened to the colour of cigarette ash by the time Jaswant left his office. On his way home, he passed cars and buses on fire, burnt shells of shops and houses billowing smoke, dead bodies of Sikhs cremated alive, bands of goondas brandishing machetes and crowbars... It was as if Partition had descended one more time. The stench of fire and smoke, the hapless victims and their remorseless tormentors, even the mob's war cry of *khoon ka badla khoon*. Everything was the same, right down to the dread rising from his soul.

He could feel the goondas' eyes probing the car as it went past. They were stopping cars at random to check if there were Sikhs inside. Many times they'd tell the driver to open the boot to make sure no Sikhs were being smuggled to safety. But they made no move to impede his progress. That he was in a government car kept them at bay. That and the fact neither he nor his driver appeared to be a Sikh.

No sooner had they entered the posh southern part of the city than the goondas melted away. The stench of fire and smoke receded. The burnt bodies and buildings disappeared...instead, there were shuttered shops and deserted streets and empty pavements… Even the dogs were not barking. It was as if someone had thrown a blanket of silence over the entire place. The silence resounded louder than all the mayhem Jaswant had witnessed. It spoke of fear and apathy.

Even though it was still evening, the first thing he did after reaching home was lock his front gate. Deepa, Savitri and Rakesh were waiting for him in the drawing room. Deepa's face was wan, her eyes puffy. Rakesh was hunched in a chair. Normally, it was hard for him to sit still. But that day he looked as if all life had been sucked out of him.

Savitri told him about the attack on the Sikh they witnessed while returning from Rakesh's school. The sheer brutality of the assault took Jaswant unawares, despite what he had seen on his way home. When Savitri came to the part where the Sikh's assailant shoved locks of his hair into his mouth, Jaswant recoiled. It was several seconds before he could find his voice.

He told them that he had no news of Prem. He had contacted one of his friends who was a superintendent in the Home Guards and stationed less than ten kilometres from Trilokpuri. His friend had promised to call him with information in the morning.

Deepa, who had been anxiously waiting for news of Prem, erupted. 'He said that and *you* accepted it?' she shouted. 'You didn't tell him to send a man

there at once? You didn't tell him that this is your
son-in-law?'

Her voice collapsed as she finished. She leapt
up from the sofa to half-run, half-stumble in the
direction of her room. Savitri went after her. Jaswant
dropped into the sofa. It pained him to see Deepa
so upset. He wished he had better news.

'Will everything be all right, Daddy?' Rakesh
asked. His voice betrayed how much he was
struggling to make sense of what was going on. It
was as if they had gone back in time and Rakesh
was a little boy all over again. A lump grew in
Jaswant's throat. He went over to embrace Rakesh.
'Don't worry, beta, everything will be all right,' he
told him. 'Now go put your mind elsewhere.'

There was a short pause before Rakesh nodded
and left for his room. Jaswant slumped on the sofa,
wishing he could feel some of the conviction with
which he had assured Rakesh that things would
work out.

His friend in the Home Guards had sent a
man to Irfan's flat. That man got nowhere near
the flat. Instead, he came back with news of a
neighbourhood under siege. An army of goondas
was running wild in Trilokpuri. They had cut all
the telephone wires and blocked the way out with
a huge concrete pipe. Near the pipe, there was a car
all smashed up. From the description, it appeared
to be Prem's. There was no sign of Prem; so there

was a chance that he had survived. But it didn't appear likely, given the evidence on hand.

He hadn't been able to look into Deepa's teary eyes and tell her the man she loved was probably dead. On the phone with Amarjeet, he had found himself just as powerless. So he had lied to both of them, saying his friend would call with news in the morning.

What was worse? The hammer blow of tragedy or the torture of not knowing?

As far as he could tell, there wasn't much to choose.

It was almost morning before Deepa gave in to sleep and Savitri could leave her room. She plodded, heavy-footed, through the house. Although she had been up all night and was aching everywhere, she had no wish to go to bed.

Jaswant was still fast asleep on the drawing-room sofa. She had found him sitting there last night when she came out of Deepa's room to get her a glass of water. He had wanted to speak to Deepa. She had talked him out of it. It would be hard for him to deal with her, given the mood she was in. Evidently, he had stayed where she left him, until fatigue got the better of him. Because of Deepa, she hadn't been able to speak to him last night. She wondered whether she should wake him up. She decided against it. Before that she needed a few moments to herself.

Opening the glass sliding doors ever so slightly, she squeezed herself out onto the front porch.

It was a morning unlike any other. There were no milkmen. No newspaper delivery boys either. No one was jogging or walking or even so much as venturing out of their front doors. The buildings looked forlorn. The trees hung their heads. The birds clustered as silently as a group of morose mourners, while the dogs went about with their barks stuck in their throats. A booming silence, of a kind that is not heard in Delhi even in the dead of the night, greeted the new day spreading itself across the sky, as bright red as a freshly inflicted wound.

It was a ghoulish silence that packed more death and grief in it than the most harrowing cries of Muharram. Within it lay the silence of the dead, the silence of the afraid, the silence of the uncaring, the silence of the ones numbed by grief... As Savitri stood in its midst, her thoughts went back to yesterday morning where her entire world had rested so snugly in its usual frame that she had not paused to give it a second thought. She had been consumed with the arrangements that needed to be made for Deepa's wedding. What she wouldn't give for that to be her only concern at that moment.

The doors behind her slid open. Jaswant came out, rubbing his eyes.

'*Ki time ho gaya hai*?' he asked.

'Just past seven.'

'I must have dropped off on the sofa,' he said with a shake of the head.

'You looked run-down last night,' Savitri said.

'How is Deepa?'

'She is sleeping.' She didn't tell him that Deepa had cried all night. With his gaunt face and drooping shoulders, he looked harrowed enough as it was.

'You should go and lie down,' he told her. 'You must be tired.'

'I will. But first you tell me what you've been hiding.'

'What do you mean?'

'We've been married for twenty-five years, Jaswant. You can't keep secrets from me.'

He looked away. For several seconds, he stood there with his eyes averted and his lips clenched in a tight line. She waited, the dread inside her growing. What was so terrible that he was finding it so hard to share it with her?

In a low voice, he revealed everything he had learned from his friend in the Home Guards. She listened quietly, catching her breath when he mentioned the state of Prem's car. There was little chance Prem would have survived. She winced as if she had been struck when he said that. She was quiet after he was finished. She had feared something like that. But learning it had actually happened was something else.

'You know all last night I was thinking of how lucky I was,' she said finally. 'I kept putting myself in Kishneet's shoes, not knowing whether her son was dead or alive. And here I was with my entire family safely home. Everything intact. And I remember thinking, *rab na kare*, if I were ever in Kishneet's situation, the one thing I would want more than anything would be to know.'

'You think I should tell them?' Jaswant asked.

'Yes.'

'We'll have to tell Deepa too.'

Savitri's face clouded. 'We'll worry about that later,' she said in a low voice.

'I'll go call Amarjeet,' he said.

She stayed where she was after he had gone. Her thoughts had jumped back several years to her early twenties when she was friends with a girl called Neelam. Neelam had got engaged to an army officer. A love-cum-arranged marriage, as Neelam put it. She and her fiancé were childhood sweethearts whose families had known each other for years. Savitri, who was grappling with being married to a man she barely knew, had been jealous.

A week before Neelam's wedding, the Chinese attacked. Neelam's fiancé was ordered to the front. He died in the ensuing battle, leaving her widowed even before she had the chance to be a bride. Savitri, who had envied Neelam until then, thanked her lucky stars that such a fate had not befallen her.

Now it appeared to have befallen her daughter.

The sliding doors scraped open. It was Jaswant. 'Prem's safe,' he announced. 'His friend Irfan just spoke to Amarjeet.' The lack of joy on his face told her there was more. 'He was badly beaten up yesterday in Trilokpuri,' Jaswant said. 'He's in bed and needs a doctor. Amarjeet is going to fetch him.'

Savitri's eyes opened wide. 'Isn't that dangerous?' she said.

'They can't just leave him there. Normally, they could have got an ambulance. But it's impossible to get one today. People are too scared to go out into the streets.'

'But he can't go all by himself!'

'No.' He paused. 'I said I'd go with him.'

The colour ebbed from Savitri's face. '*Ki tussi paagal ho gaye ho*?' she said.

'Savitri…'

'You know the gadar going on outside…'

'Savitri, Prem is going to be our son-in-law. He is hurt. We must do what we can for him.'

'Don't you lecture me, I'm not going to risk losing my husband.'

Her eyes were gleaming with tears. He took her in his arms and held her close. He had to do this for Deepa, he told her. He implored her to have faith, no harm would come to him. She didn't utter a word, simply held on to him as tightly as she could. In the end, he was the one who stepped back. He lingered for a few seconds, looking like he wanted to say something. Then he swung around and went back inside without uttering a word. She remained where she was, gazing after him.

Jaswant looked in on Deepa and Rakesh before leaving. They were both asleep. He was struck by how drawn Deepa's face appeared, even in sleep. He hoped to have some news that would cheer her up by the time she woke up.

Savitri had come back inside and was slumped on the drawing-room sofa. Once again, he told her to have faith, things would turn out fine. Even as he was speaking, he realized how trite his words must have been sounding to her at the moment. He couldn't think of anything else to tell her. She didn't utter a word. She didn't appear to have even heard him. He went out to his car, afraid his resolve might crack if he stayed there any longer.

The streets were empty. Normally, such a sight would have been welcome. That day, it was disturbing. The sound of the Fiat going down the deserted road resounded like a roar. Curious eyes watched from the windows and balconies of flats and houses. They were probably wondering why he was out there. Was he stupid or mad or both? Jaswant kept his eyes fastened to the road. To his right and left he could make out vandalized shops, walls blaring hate graffiti, the charred remains of cars and bicycles… Still, it wasn't as bad as he had feared. His part of Delhi, at least, had escaped the worst of the nightmare.

Amarjeet was waiting when he reached Shanti Niketan. Jaswant could barely recognize him. Amarjeet had discarded his kara and shaved off his beard. His hair was also cut much closer to the scalp than Jaswant remembered. The anxiety under which he had been labouring since yesterday morning showed all over his face. Jaswant made out lines as deep as cracks, dark circles hemming in the eyes, a tremor in the jaw… Even the voice in which Amarjeet said hello sounded strangled.

They decided to take Amarjeet's car. It was bigger than Jaswant's and had a full tank of petrol. With no petrol pump likely to be open, they couldn't run the risk of running low. They combed the car for anything that might give away the fact that Amarjeet was a Sikh. Jaswant had a picture of Ram and Sita in his car. He pasted it to the dashboard of Amarjeet's Ambassador and took the wheel himself; he could see Amarjeet was in no shape to drive.

Once they were on their way, Amarjeet revealed what he had learnt from Irfan in a tremulous voice. Prem had been kept sedated through the night as the goondas ran amok all over Trilokpuri. The night had been full of yelling and screaming and the sound of things being smashed. The stench of smoke and burning flesh wafted all over the neighbourhood. No one got a moment's sleep as they sat quaking in their homes. When Irfan came out of Raj Kumar's flat in the morning, he found vultures feasting on dead bodies. The goondas had bludgeoned people to death, burnt them alive, looted their homes, raped their women... A local politician had led them and there was at least one policeman in their ranks. What was more, they seemed to know where all the Sikhs lived.

To Jaswant it sounded like Partition all over again. It wasn't fair that he should have to go through something like that twice in one lifetime.

His mood darkened further as they passed through Central and East Delhi. Dead bodies, charred beyond recognition, lay about in the streets. Several had hair sticking out of their mouths. Locks of hair were adrift on the road, perhaps looking for the heads from whom they had been split so cruelly. There were remains of cars and bicycles, shops torched black, gurudwaras razed to the ground. They went past a house, where each of the five steps rising to the front door was smeared with blood. On the wall next to the front door someone had drawn a cross in chalk. Later, Jaswant would learn that was a sign to tell the mob that it was a Sikh home.

Air swelling with the anguish of unfulfilled souls not ready to leave the earth hammered on the car as it wound a tortuous path towards Trilokpuri.

The lines on Amarjeet's face grew deeper and his eyes glimmered with tears as he took in the horrors they were passing. Jaswant, painfully conscious of the queasiness prodding his stomach, kept his eyes glued to the road, trying to see as little of the horror as possible.

Finally, they were in Trilokpuri. With the help of the other residents, Irfan had removed the concrete pipe from the dirt track. What was left of Prem's car lay in pieces.

What they had witnessed so far was nothing compared to the horrors awaiting them in Trilokpuri. No sooner had they entered the neighbourhood than the stench of rotting flesh assailed their nostrils. Dead bodies lay about in the gutters, in the alleyways, in the balconies of flats. Smoke still came off the burnt corpses scattered on the ground, while an ashen cloud hovered above the neighbourhood, blocking the sun. Hair lay piled up next to the corpses. The shrieks of the vultures swooping down for their feast rent the air, drowning out the wails of the mourners.

There were so many dead bodies in the way of the car that they were forced to get out and make their way on foot. Out in the open, the din was louder, the stench sharper, the smoke more pungent... Their eyes smarted and they were forced to cover their noses with their handkerchiefs.

From the other side of a car window, the dead had

formed a part of the monstrous tableau streaming past. Now they no longer had that anonymity. They announced themselves in one slow, stomach-churning close-up after another. Their proximity gave them shape and definition. They were no longer a succession of broken limbs and charred faces, but recognizable as men who could have been fathers, grandfathers, sons, brothers, husbands... women who had loved and been loved... people who'd had hopes and ambitions... now they were merely cold corpses lying about in the streets of a neighbourhood that had been their home.

It was much later that Jaswant experienced the full horror of that walk through Trilokpuri. That morning, he plodded through its alleyways like a sleepwalker, far too anxious about Prem to comprehend the horrors he was witnessing. In memory, that moment came back stripped of his concern for Prem. Without the merciful veil of worry, he could make out so much more than he had consciously registered at the moment. Each charred face, each broken limb. The way he recoiled as he stepped on a corpse. How bile filled his throat as the smell of death invaded him.

It was an eternity before the walk was over and they were at Raj Kumar's flat. Prem was fully conscious and sitting up in bed. The bandage on his head was disconcerting, as was his bloated jaw. But at least he was alive. Amarjeet, unable to restrain himself any longer, wept as he embraced him. Jaswant, Irfan and Raj Kumar left them alone in the room. Jaswant asked after Prem's injuries. Raj Kumar was in the midst of explaining them when Amarjeet emerged from the room and said they'd better go home right away.

Prem was still weak from the blood he had lost. Amarjeet decided he should not walk. The four of them carried him to the car, where they made him as comfortable as they could in the backseat. Amarjeet thanked Irfan and Raj Kumar. Embracing Irfan, he told him that if he ever needed his help he simply had to ask.

They started for home. Jaswant drove slowly, trying to spare Prem any bumps. Prem began to relate what had happened. Amarjeet interrupted him. All that could wait. Right now Prem needed to save his energy for the long drive home.

They had been on the road for ten minutes when they found their path blocked. Several men had collected in the middle of the road. They were brandishing lathis, crowbars and bicycle chains while motioning for the car to stop. They had chosen a spot where the road veered sharply to the left and there was nowhere to turn. Jaswant had no choice but to stop. There was no way he could drive through them.

'Let me do the talking,' he told Prem and Amarjeet.

He rolled down his window. A tall young man with a crowbar, dressed in a pair of jeans and a checked shirt, came over. The others gathered round him. The man peered inside the car, his eyes zeroing in on Prem.

'What happened to him?' he demanded.

'He is my son,' Jaswant said. 'A Sikh chootiya hit him. He was out like all of you, avenging Indiraji. The saala got him from behind. My brother and I are taking him home from the doctor.'

One of the other men was nodding. 'Yes, that is what those maaderchods are like,' he said. 'They stab you in the back. That is exactly what they did to Indiraji. Those bodyguards had taken an oath to protect her. And then they turned around and shot her in cold blood.'

There was a chorus of agreement. The man with the crowbar was not convinced.

'How do we know that you are not lying?' he said. 'You could be Sikhs trying to flee.'

'*Kya baat karte ho, dekho,*' Jaswant pointed to the picture on the dashboard. 'We are Ram bhakts. How can we be Sikhs?'

The man didn't say anything. The expression on his face, though, suggested he was still not convinced. Again his gaze travelled over Prem. Jaswant's mouth felt as if he had swallowed sawdust. His stomach was as tight as a drum. It appeared his bluff was not working.

Suddenly, there was a shout. The men turned around. 'Look, here's Jagat,' one of them cried out.

A heavily built man in a blue kurta-pyjama had emerged from one of the houses next to the road. He was dragging a naked boy behind him. A sari-clad woman was trailing the two of them, pleading with the man to let the boy go.

'Look what I found,' the man said. 'The saali had dressed the little pup in a girl's clothes. She thought that way she could fool us.'

'Please spare my son,' the woman begged. 'He's all I have. My husband is already dead. *Rab de vaaste* let him go.'

The men began to drift away from the car.

'You can go,' the man with the crowbar told Jaswant.

The woman had spotted the car. 'Save my son,' she shouted. 'Please, sahib, he's all I have.'

The man with the crowbar was eyeing Jaswant. 'For god's sake, chalo,' Amarjeet muttered. Jaswant gritted his teeth and started the engine. The woman continued to shout after them as they drove away.

Save my son, she screamed.

Her keening voice lunged at Jaswant like a knife, plunging through skin and bone to raise shivers worse than anything he had felt even on a freezing December morning. Her pinched face loomed in front of him. Her eyes were squeezed shut, as she reached into the depths of her desperation to hurl her most soul-shattering scream at him. Her long hair hung ragged on her shoulders and flailing arms. *Save my son! Save my son! Save my son!*

He sat up in bed with a gasp. He was trembling all over. His face was leaking sweat. His frantic eyes darted around the room. Where was she? All he could make out were the familiar sights of his bedroom; the old white sheet collected round his legs, Savitri stretched out under her sheet next to him, the white face of the wall clock opposite, telling him it was three in the morning…

His eyes stopped moving as he realized he had been dreaming. He dried his face with his handkerchief and climbed out of bed, taking care not to disturb Savitri. Throwing on a red dressing gown, he made his way to the drawing room. There, he switched on the light and settled in the sofa.

For three nights she had been screaming.

The day's newspaper lay on the table in front of him. He looked through it, before leafing through the magazines lying beside it. His mind was too scrambled to grasp what any of them had to say. Before long, he gave up and slumped back in the sofa.

Tonight he should have been able to sleep. For the first time since the assassination, the government seemed serious about cracking down on the rioters. The army had been deployed in Delhi. Jawans were conducting flag marches in the streets. Curfew had been imposed and camps set up to help the riot victims. The news about Prem was encouraging. The swelling in his face was subsiding, which meant there was no fracture. His other wounds were healing as well. Deepa and Prem had talked over the phone. For the first time in days, there was a smile on Deepa's face... But he still found it impossible to sleep. The moment he closed his eyes, he ran into the woman beseeching him to save her son.

She was a young woman, possibly in her mid-twenties. He hadn't seen enough of her to gauge her circumstances, but she had to be lower middle-class if she lived on that street. If she worked anywhere, it was in a low-paying job. She would have struggled to make ends meet even when her husband was alive and working. Now, with her husband dead and in all probability her son as well, she would struggle to stay afloat. Her life's anchors had been yanked from under her. There was nothing to save her from sinking.

He had kept telling himself that he had done the right thing; that anyone else in his place would have acted no differently. The woman was a stranger. His first responsibility was to the man his daughter was going to marry. Furthermore, even Amarjeet had prompted him to get going and forget about her; Amarjeet, who was a Sikh like the woman. Then, it was debatable whether they could have helped her even if they had tried. Those men had them outnumbered and outgunned.

At times, that argument was enough for him to ignore her screams.

There were other times when none of that logic held up; when all he could see was the woman's desperate face; when her voice resounded in every part of him, making the hairs stand on the back of his neck.

The starry night sky was framed in the window in front of him. Tonight what had happened would be sinking in all over Delhi. Now that the madness was over, the time had come for stock-taking. Sikh families would be reeling from the absence of loved ones, sifting through the ashes of a lifetime's work gone up in smoke... There would be some drowning in the relief of coming through the riots unscathed. But not too many. Relief would be a trickle compared to the deluge of anger and despair.

His gaze drifted to the part of the sky that stretched to the south. The Kohlis lived in that direction. Amarjeet and he had spoken briefly since that day in Trilokpuri. It had all been about how Prem was doing. Until now, Amarjeet had been consumed with Prem and surviving the riots. Tonight he would be free from those concerns.

What was he thinking?

* * *

Over in Shanti Niketan, Amarjeet was going over the house for the third time to make sure all the doors and windows were securely fastened. A deep sense of fear had him in its grip, even though the danger had eased with the deployment of the army.

It was a while before he was satisfied enough to make his way to his room and pour himself a peg of whisky. Seema and Kishneet were in bed. He had given Prem a tablet to help him sleep. The last time he checked, it was doing its job. He ought to be in bed himself, but he simply could not fall asleep. Sleep had deserted him since the day they had brought Prem home from Trilokpuri.

He downed the drink, after which he poured himself another and leaned back in his chair to sip slowly. Right through the evening, Kishneet and he had argued. She was adamant they should leave India as soon as possible. This time, they had escaped, in Prem's case barely. Next time, they may not be so lucky. They had good friends in the Sikh community in Seattle. They should contact them immediately and move.

At first, Amarjeet had laughed off the idea. That did not faze Kishneet in the least. She had doggedly persisted with her mantra. In the end, Amarjeet had lost his temper and shouted at her, demanding to know if she knew what she was saying. She was telling him to give up a lifetime's work and start again in a foreign country.

'What's the point of having everything when you can't be safe?' Kishneet had retorted. At least, in another country they would not have to live with fear hanging over their heads. She had accused him of thinking only of himself. He was so preoccupied with what he would lose that he hadn't given the children a thought. What kind of future would they have in an India that equated them with the killers of its prime minister?

It had been a while before she had left him alone, far too exhausted to argue any more. By then, enough of what she was saying had clawed its way into Amarjeet. While he still baulked at the idea of starting again in another country, he had to agree that she had a point when it came to the children. Prem had already been attacked. While he was trying to be brave, it was apparent that he was badly shaken. And Seema had been scarred by what had happened even though she had escaped physical harm. Since that hateful phone call, she hadn't spoken much. Even having Prem back had failed to raise her spirits. Furthermore, what kind of life would Prem and Seema have in a place where their religion made them targets?

He fingered the light stubble on his face. The beard was growing back. The fact that he had to shave it off still rankled. Yes, he had cut his kesh a long time ago. But that was his choice. The beard he was forced to shed. Would his children have to live like that, constantly hiding a part of themselves in order to survive? And even that did not guarantee survival. The woman they had encountered while bringing Prem home from Trilokpuri hadn't been able to protect her son, despite dressing him in girls' clothes.

On the other side of the window, to his right, the garden stretched in darkness. Beyond it was the boundary wall, and then the city. Thirty-seven years ago, he had arrived there with little more than the clothes on his back. His first home was a tent in a refugee camp which he had shared with his extended family. Much of his childhood had been spent among people who talked about nothing except what they had lost. Fired by the desire not to end up like them, he had worked his way up from a tent in a refugee camp to living in one of the city's finest neighbourhoods and hobnobbing with its elite. Now, in the blink of an eye, he had been flung back thirty-seven years, once again contemplating flight, as the city that had given him refuge shrieked for his blood.

He finished his drink and rose stiffly to make his way to bed. He paused outside Prem's room, thinking he had heard something. For several seconds he stood still, listening. He couldn't make out a sound. Finally, he continued on his way.

* * *

Prem tensed at the sound of footfalls in the hallway outside his room. Was that his father making his way to bed? Abruptly, the footfalls ceased. Amarjeet had stopped. Was he going to come in? Prem's body stiffened. Then the footfalls resumed. Soon, there was the sound of a door opening and closing.

The tightness in Prem's body dissipated. He had just woken up screaming, though, today, he had been able to stop himself just in time. For that much he was grateful. The last two nights, he had woken up the entire house.

It seemed those four men were waiting for him each time he closed his eyes; waiting with their taunting faces and maniacal laughter to deliver the blows that flooded him with pain.

He ran his tongue over his dry lips. Until that morning, he'd had a bandage that went around his head. That morning, it had shrunk to a piece of sticking plaster covering one half of his forehead. While it looked bad, the bruise did not hurt. The swelling in the jaw was far more painful. He still found it difficult to chew or sleep on that side.

Still, he should count himself lucky. He only had to recall the woman they ran into on their way back from Trilokpuri. She had lost her husband and, most probably her son, in the riots. He, on the other hand, was home and surrounded by people who cared for him.

He had been overrun by love and sympathy since his return. His family had fallen over themselves to take care of him. Deepa had called several times. She had even wanted to visit. She abandoned the idea only after he told her not to be foolish, he was in good hands.

But none of that had allowed him to forget. He doubted if he ever could.

The first thing Amarjeet did, the morning after the curfew was lifted, was despatch Vishnu to round up workmen who would rub out his name from the nameplate next to the front gate and replace it with the street address. He told Vishnu to get Sikh or Muslim workmen for the job. After what had happened, he could not bring himself to trust an unknown Hindu.

Neither he, nor anyone else in his family, ventured out of the house in the next few days. They even visited the garden in the dark. They would steal back into the house at the slightest hint of a disturbance. Through Vishnu, they stocked up on food and medicines as if under siege. Vishnu would unlock the front gate to let the maid into the compound in the morning. He'd lock it up again the moment she left.

When the Kohlis finally emerged, it was with trepidation. Amarjeet carpooled with his Sikh neighbours to and from his clinic, which had survived the violence. He made sure he was home well before dark. Only after a few days of this did he and Kishneet consider it safe for Seema to return to school. That, too, after they and their

Sikh neighbours had established a carpool for their school-going children. By then Amarjeet had got the boundary wall surrounding the house raised several inches. He'd also had steel spikes and crushed glass installed on top of the wall.

His concern, however, failed to dissolve as he found himself wondering what more he could do to protect his family. Nothing appeared to satisfy Kishneet. She continued to bombard him with her idea of leaving India as soon as possible. 'How long can we live like this?' she'd demand, before going on to paint a new doomsday scenario. Not knowing what to tell her, Amarjeet would simply keep quiet and look away. Her doomsday scenarios continued to feed the unease gnawing at him.

Seema, on the other hand, was grappling with a different demon. Despite her best efforts, she had been unable to wrench her thoughts away from the horrible man who had threatened to kill them on the phone. For a while, her concern for Prem had pushed him into the background. But he returned as Prem got better.

His voice had brimmed with the kind of hate you'd expect from a sworn enemy. And he didn't even know them!

She mulled that over for a few days. Finally, she asked Amarjeet. He stared at her. 'There are people who hate you for who you are,' he said finally, in a voice he hadn't used with her since she was in primary school.

She was taken aback. In her mind, you had to harm someone for them to hate you. That man was a stranger. Yet he hated them enough to want to kill them. 'They hate you even if you've done nothing to harm them?' she said in a low voice.

Amarjeet, realizing what a shock this was for her, put his arm round her shoulders. 'Yes,' he said. 'Who you are is enough for some people to want to hurt you.'

She didn't say anything. She was still finding it hard to believe. He asked if she was okay. She nodded mechanically. He went away with a pat on her back.

The memory of the phone call stayed with her when she went back to school. Everything about school was different. She was no longer riding in the school bus with her friends. She was going back and forth with people she barely knew; people with whom the only thing she had in common was her religion. That wasn't enough to make up for the years spent growing up together. The ride seemed to take forever as she sat in morose silence in one corner of the car

Most of the Sikh boys at school had shed their patkas and turbans. They had also cut their hair and shaved off what beard they had. A Sikh teacher had done the same. It was strange to see so many familiar faces suddenly become unfamiliar. But then, that had happened at home too, with her father.

What would stay with her was the manner in which those few days of mayhem had washed away years of togetherness. Students in her class would turn away the instant they saw her. Less than a month ago, the same boys and girls had been greeting her pleasantly and borrowing her class notes. Even the girls she had been thick with had become different. Their conversation was far from effortless. It sounded more like an affectation, with everybody doing their damnedest not to say anything the least bit contentious. Everyone told her how sorry they were for what had happened to Prem. But the fact they saw the riots differently made her doubt their sincerity. 'The Sikhs had it coming after killing Mrs Gandhi,' she heard one of her friends tell the rest of the group. The friend obviously thought she was well out of earshot at the moment. Nobody repudiated her. Rather, there were murmurs of agreement.

Rakesh, who did not change, disturbed her for a completely different reason. Even the fact that Prem had been beaten and almost killed seemed to have left no lasting impact on him. He acted as if the whole experience was like a passing storm, after which everything had gone back to the way it always was. The two of them were invariably thrown together when their families met in each other's homes. In the past, they had been happy to retreat together and gossip about school, books,

Hindi movies and television serials. Now she found herself incapable of such chitchat; it appeared trite in the world she was inhabiting. Rakesh couldn't figure out why she wasn't responding with the same enthusiasm. His face would scream, *What's wrong with you?*

As the days passed, she began to retreat into herself. She spoke only when she was addressed. Otherwise, she was content to interact with her thoughts, none of which were bright or happy. She rarely left home, except to go to school and, at home too, she spent most of her time alone in her room. Ordinarily, such behaviour would have rung alarm bells. But Amarjeet and Kishneet were far too occupied with the hostile environment to notice, and Prem was busy with his own demons.

Prem headed straight for the gurudwara on the first day he left the house. By now, all that was left of his bruises was a cut on the forehead that was covered by a piece of sticking plaster. The swelling on his face had subsided and he could move about without any discomfort. The taunting faces of those four men, however, loomed large in his thoughts. They continued to beset his sleep, often keeping him up until the early hours of the morning. It had come to a point where he was scared to fall asleep and was attempting to stay awake for as long as possible. The lack of sleep, coupled with his pressing need to evade those men, had given his face a hunted look, and his eyes never remained still.

When he reached the gurudwara, he found it razed to the ground. The front gate lay in pieces. The board on which the gurudwara's name was written had been ripped off and hammered to smithereens. The boundary wall was scarified with hate graffiti calling Sikhs all kinds of names while predicting dire consequences for them if they didn't 'behave' themselves.

He had passed two other gurudwaras that had

met with a similar fate on his way. Yet he was shocked to see the place. He drifted, wide-eyed, like someone in a trance, before making his way to where a crowd of grim-faced men had collected on the gurudwara grounds. He didn't recognize them at first glance. Then he realized that they were regular visitors to the gurudwara who had been forced to cut their hair during the riots in order to survive. He hadn't recognized them without their beards and turbans. The prematurely elderly man at the centre of the crowd was the head granthi.

The granthi had aged several years in a matter of days. A middle-aged man, now he appeared wizened. His right arm was in a sling. There was a bruise on the part of his forehead that showed outside his turban and the colour had vanished from his face.

'I tried to stop them,' he was saying. 'But they wouldn't listen. They were hell-bent on burning it down. Finally, I asked them to at least let me take the Guru Granth Sahib out of the gurudwara. I got down on my knees and begged. They simply laughed. "You old fool," one of them said. "You are lucky we are sparing your life. Get out before we change our minds."

'They set the whole place on fire. Everything burned, everything. I tried to run in and save what I could. For that they gave me this.'

He showed them the arm in a sling and pointed

to the bruise on his forehead with his good arm. There was a rumble in the crowd as voices rose in anger. The granthi called for silence by holding up his good arm.

'Brothers, before you do anything else you must restore the gurudwara to its rightful glory,' he said. 'We will start rebuilding tomorrow. As Sikhs it is your duty to be part of that process. Please be here for kar sewa.'

The men nodded, saying they'd certainly come. The crowd began to disperse. One man came up to Prem.

'*Sat sri akal,* Premji,' he said. It was Surjit.

* * *

Surjit suggested they go talk somewhere else. It was far too depressing to sit there, surrounded by the burnt walls of the gurudwara. He said he knew a place nearby that made good chai.

The place he had in mind was a dhaba located close to the gurudwara. As they walked towards it, they were stopped and frisked by an armed policeman. Surjit appeared to be used to that. 'Here we go again,' he said, when the policeman told them to stop.

At the dhaba, they settled at a table placed next to the road. Prem stood out from the other customers in his clean, pressed shirt and slacks. He appeared distinctly uncomfortable as he sat rigidly near the edge of the chair. It was a flimsy plastic chair and he was scared it might collapse any moment. The posse of flies that had trailed them from the gurudwara didn't help matters. He worried that one of them would fall into his chai. The chai, too, was delivered in a glass instead of a cup. When he picked up the glass, he almost cried out because it was so hot. It was a while before he could bring himself to sip the chai. He grimaced the instant he tasted it. It was far too sweet.

Surjit, on the other hand, was spread out in his chair with his legs splayed in front of him. He exchanged greetings with the other men in the dhaba; evidently he knew them well. When his chai arrived, he devoured it with smacking sounds, happily swatting away flies when they buzzed too close to him. The sweet, scalding hot chai was far more to his taste than the coffee he had barely touched at Nirula's.

Prem related what had happened in Trilokpuri. Surjit did not interrupt him. After Prem was finished, he remained quiet for several seconds.

'I don't know one Sikh in Delhi who was not swept up in the riots,' he said finally. 'Either like you they were attacked personally, or someone close to them was. People have lost relatives, loved ones. They have seen a lifetime's earnings go up in smoke.'

He shook his head with his lips pressed together.

'You know what I find most interesting about these riots?' he said. 'It is how quickly they ended. The moment the army was called in the rioters disappeared, like jadoo, almost as if they had vanished into thin air.'

He snorted. 'What do these people think we are? Idiots? If this doesn't prove that the riots were organized by the government then what does? First, they decided we needed to be taught a lesson and sprang those goondas on us. Once they thought we'd had enough, they pulled the goondas off and dumped them back into the very hole from which they had fished them out.'

He threw a glance round the dhaba before leaning forward to say, in a low voice, 'Last time you told me you couldn't be with us because of a girl. Now the government has waged war on Sikhs. Can you still go on living your life as if nothing has happened?'

A voice inside Prem was telling him to walk away from there as fast as he could.

'Can you?' Surjit's voice jabbed at him.

But there were also those taunting faces, their laughter ringing in his ears as he cringed at the memory of their blows.

'No,' he said.

Surjit smiled. 'Good. Very good.'

He rose to his feet. 'I'll be in touch,' he said before leaving.

The Kwality restaurant was deserted that evening. The headwaiter, who knew Jaswant after years of him patronizing the place, told him it was like that every evening. Lunch was still strong, he said as he led Jaswant to a table by the window, but people were staying home after dark.

Jaswant could see the street outside packed with traffic and pedestrians on their way home. Several shops had already closed, although the clock hadn't struck six yet. Others were in the process of downing their shutters. The hawkers, the shoeshine boys and the pavement news-stand-wallahs were rolling up their wares. There were armed policemen wherever one looked. In a few hours it would be impossible to drive without running into a police checkpoint every few miles.

How much the world had changed from when he had visited the restaurant with Pritam in June. It was hard to believe that was less than six months ago.

Once again, he was there to meet Pritam, who had phoned in the morning to say he needed to see him. He couldn't do lunch, but he was game for a cup of tea in the evening. Jaswant agreed. He was intrigued by Pritam's desire to meet and that too as soon as possible. He tried quizzing him about it, but Pritam simply said he'd tell him everything when they met.

He rose to his feet as he saw Pritam, in a dark suit with a red tie. He was carrying a black briefcase that he placed on the carpet next to his chair. The two of them greeted each other with a warm handshake. 'How are you?' Jaswant asked, after the waiter had left.

'How do you think I would be in these times?' Pritam said. 'My wife worries the moment I leave home, even though I'm a cut Sikh with a government job. She imagines all kinds of terrible things if I don't ring her every two hours. No other Sikh I know ventures out alone. They ride to work with at least three other Sikhs and firearms in the car. My wife thinks I should do the same. I tell her that's impossible, given the nature of my job. Then resign, she says. Every day I get calls from estate agents wanting to know when I'm selling my house. *When!* Not *if.* Since I'm a Sikh, they are sure I'll leave Delhi sooner or later.'

Jaswant pursed his lips. As a Hindu, he was embarrassed and saddened by what Pritam had just told him even though it was hardly unexpected.

Pritam opened the black briefcase to extract a manila envelope that he handed to Jaswant. 'I wanted you to see this,' he said.

The envelope contained a black-and-white picture of two men having chai at a dhaba. Jaswant caught his breath as he recognized one of them as Prem.

'That's Deepa's fiancé Prem, isn't it?' Pritam said.

Jaswant nodded.

'I thought it was him when I saw the picture,' Pritam said. 'I remembered him from Deepa's engagement party.'

'Who is the man with him?' Jaswant asked.

'He goes by several names. In the gurudwara your damaad visits, he is called Surjit. Since the assassination we have increased our surveillance in the gurudwaras. You know, the plot to kill Mrs Gandhi was hatched in one of them? So now I have double the number of informers and undercover men working there. One of them took this picture. He was tailing Surjit. He has standing orders to tell me about everyone Surjit meets, especially young men. You see, Surjit is close to the militants. He may very well be in the business of recruiting for them.'

He paused. 'I am telling you this as a friend, Jaswant,' he said. 'Deepa is like a daughter to me. I would hate to see anything bad happen to her. But…'

He looked at the picture in Jaswant's hands.

* * *

Jaswant left the restaurant in a daze. He was almost run over by a car on his way to the parking lot. It screeched to a halt just a few inches from him. The irate driver told him off in no uncertain terms. He raised a hand in apology and hurried over to where his car was parked.

Prem mixed up with militants! He couldn't have imagined such a thing in his wildest dreams. Something like it could ruin his career. Not to speak of his family's future. In a climate where people were being locked up on the mere suspicion of being close to the militants, he'd be lucky to get his pension. Then the social disgrace, the loss of face...

The drive home was tortuous. He found it hard to concentrate on the road. At one point, he almost ran into the back of a bus. He was relieved to finally pull up in his driveway. After entering the house, he headed straight for the master bedroom where he collapsed on the bed.

By now the initial shock had passed and he was kicking himself for not figuring things out earlier. The signs had been there for everyone to see. Prem had grown his hair and beard. He had started visiting the gurudwara... Oh, how could he have been so blind? He should have put his foot down when Savitri first mentioned the proposal.

'You didn't even come to say hello to me,' Savitri's voice sounded. She sat down next to him on the bed. One look was all she needed to surmise that something was wrong. '*Ki gal hai*?' she asked

'I don't quite know how to tell you,' he said.

'Kyun? What happened?'

He related everything he had learned from Pritam. 'Thank god the information fell in Pritam's hands,' he said, after he was finished. 'He'll at least bury it long enough for me to get everything in order. If it were a stranger...' He shuddered. 'We have to break off this engagement immediately,' he said.

'Let's not be hasty,' Savitri told him.

His eyes widened. 'Not be hasty? *Tussi ki gal kar rahe ho*? How long do you think it'll be before someone else gets to know? I'm a government servant. I can't...'

'I am simply saying we shouldn't do something we will regret later.'

Disbelief broke out all over Jaswant's face. 'Surely you don't think this marriage can still go ahead?' he said. 'If we let Deepa marry this boy now, we will not simply be paagal, we'll be criminal in our negligence. Not only will our daughter's life be ruined, it'll be curtains for the entire family.'

Savitri let out a long sigh. 'I understand what you're saying,' she said. 'But Deepa loves Prem. Before we do anything, we have to talk to her. I'm sure she knows nothing about this. It'll come as a big shock to her.'

Jaswant reflected on Savitri's words. He had to admit she made sense.

'Okay, but we don't have much time,' he said. 'Right now Pritam is sitting on the information. I don't know how long he can do that.'

'I'll talk to her tonight,' Savitri told him.

* * *

Dinner that night was a quiet affair. Rakesh was impatient to be done as quickly as possible so that he could park himself in front of the TV for the highlights from the India–Pakistan Test series. Jaswant and Savitri were busy waiting for Deepa to finish, so that Savitri could take her aside and talk to her. Deepa appeared wrapped up in her own thoughts as she picked at her food. When she was done, she said she was going to her room to read a book. Savitri waited a few minutes before following her. She found Deepa lying in bed and staring at the ceiling.

'You are not reading your book?' she said.

'I was going to,' Deepa said, sitting up in bed. 'I just thought I'd lie down for a few minutes.'

Her eyes had been wide open. She had been thinking rather than resting. It was obvious she had something on her mind. Normally, Savitri would have asked what it was. But that night she had other things to attend to.

She dragged the chair from the desk over to the bed and settled in it.

'Deepa, today your father met Pritam uncle,' she began. She told Deepa about Jaswant's conversation with Pritam. The expression on Deepa's face changed from mild curiosity to incredulity.

'I don't believe this,' she said after Savitri was finished. 'Prem would never get mixed up in something like this.'

'Beta, Pritam uncle showed…'

'I don't care how many pictures Pritam uncle showed Daddy. What does that picture prove, anyways? That Prem had chai with someone? That doesn't mean he's mixed up with militants.'

'Beta…'

'Mummy, I'm surprised that you and Daddy can even think of something like that.'

'Beta…'

'I can say for sure Prem would never do that. I know him.'

'You *do not* know him,' Savitri snapped. 'You look at him and you see the boy you fell in love with, because that's what you want to see. He's no longer that boy. He's different now. In your heart of hearts you know that.'

Deepa's mouth was trembling. Her face looked stricken. Savitri rose to sit down next to her on the bed. Taking Deepa's hand in hers, she said, 'We are your parents, Deepa. We can't sit by and see your life go down the toilet. This is serious.'

Deepa didn't say anything.

Deepa had expected to see Prem that afternoon. He was supposed to visit her after work. Around two o'clock, he had rung to say he couldn't make it. He had to meet someone. When Deepa had asked who it was, he was mysterious, simply telling her that it was someone she did not know. He had promised to phone in the evening. He never did.

She was perturbed by his reluctance to tell her who he was meeting. When he did not phone, she became even more concerned. She had been lying in bed, wondering who he could be seeing, when Savitri had come into her room.

After Savitri left, she reflected on what she had learnt. Prem in league with the militants! There was a time when she would have dismissed that out of hand. Now she could not say. Savitri was right. He had changed. There were still times when he revealed glimpses of his old self and, for a while, it seemed they were back in the days right after their engagement; their brief spring of happiness before the summer descended with its horror. But those moments were now as rare as a soothing drizzle in the middle of a blazing hot summer day. Most of the time, they resembled an old couple who had run out of things to say to each other and were staying together out of sheer habit, rather than two young people about to get married.

She had wanted to believe that this state of affairs was temporary. Prem had been through a lot. Given time, he'd go back to being himself and then everything would return to the way it was, just like it had after his outburst in Nehru Park. What she had learnt from Savitri told her how far-fetched that notion was. The man she had fallen in love with was gone, to be replaced by a stranger with whom she could never hope to connect.

She didn't sleep a moment that night. In the morning, Jaswant and Savitri eyed her expectantly at the breakfast table. She avoided their eyes as she picked at her food. She could sense their impatience. Last night, she had told Savitri that she'd give her an answer in the morning.

'I've thought everything over,' she said finally. 'I love Prem, but if he is involved with the militants then I won't marry him.'

Her voice crumbled as she finished. Tears shone in her eyes. Savitri squeezed her hand. Jaswant looked relieved.

'But I have to speak to him first,' she said.

The relief on Jaswant's face was replaced by disbelief. 'What is there to talk about?' he demanded. 'All that is left is for me to get in touch with Amarjeet and call the whole thing off.'

'No, I must talk to him.'

'What is there to talk about?'

'I want to know why he's thrown away our life together.'

'Deepa, you are being impossible.'

'Daddy…'

'Deepa, go to your room. Let me talk to your father,' Savitri interrupted.

She could see things were about to get out of hand. Deepa gave her a stricken look before leaving.

'What's wrong in letting her talk to him?' she said after Deepa was gone.

'What do you mean?' Jaswant said.

'It's only logical. The two of them have a relationship. She can't just end it, without even speaking to him. We didn't arrange this marriage, Jaswant. So we can't just break it off.'

From the way he ground his teeth, she could tell he was running out of patience. 'All right,' he said finally, 'but she had better do it soon.'

He rose to go to work. Savitri went to Deepa's room, where she found her in tears. She tried to comfort her the best she could, even though she knew she could do little. She knew that in the future, Deepa would look back at that moment and thank her lucky stars for what had happened. But right now all she could do was mourn her moribund dream of sharing her life with Prem.

* * *

It was almost an hour before Deepa was composed enough to phone Prem at the Oberoi. He was unable to come on the line. The man who answered the phone told her he had said he'd call back.

He never did. When he still hadn't rung by lunchtime, Deepa decided to go to the Oberoi herself. Prem would be getting off work soon. She'd speak to him then.

Savitri insisted on accompanying her, promising not to get involved in any way. 'I'll sit and wait for you in the lobby,' she said. She wanted to be close by; Deepa was sure to need comforting at the end of her conversation with Prem. Deepa wasn't keen on taking her. It took some convincing on Savitri's part to change her mind.

The two of them left in the Fiat right after lunch. Deepa didn't utter a word the entire way. Savitri tried telling her what had happened was fortuitous. If she had married Prem, they would have been in a real mess. It was exactly what she had said in the morning. She didn't expect her words to help any more than they had in the morning. But she still repeated them. She couldn't bear to see Deepa being miserable, without making an effort to help.

It wasn't long before they were near the Oberoi. Deepa suddenly spotted Prem on the pavement outside. 'There he is,' she pointed. He had his back to them. As Savitri brought the car to a stop, Deepa shouted after him, but he didn't turn around. She jumped out, leaving Savitri to turn into the hotel's driveway.

Prem was crossing the street. He was still dressed in his waiter's uniform, which was strange. Normally, he changed out of it right after work. Moreover, where was he walking to? Since the incident in Trilokpuri, Amarjeet had his driver drive him to and from work. She set off after him.

A sudden flurry of traffic kept her on the pavement, her agitated feet moving forward and back as she waited for a break in the traffic while tossing anxious glances at Prem, who was steadily making his way to the bus stop up the street. Finally, there was a break in the traffic and she could rush across the street.

By the time she got to the bus stop, Prem had just boarded a bus. There was a jostling crowd still waiting to board it. There was plenty of shoving, but she gritted her teeth and edged forward the best she could. She was just able to get on before the bus wheezed ahead.

Only then did she wonder what Prem was doing in a bus.

The day before, Prem had received a call from Surjit at work. From the sound of traffic in the background, he could tell Surjit was calling from a public telephone booth. He wanted Prem to go to the Lodhi Gardens right after work. When he got there, he was to make his way to the Bara Gumbad, where someone would be waiting for him. Prem asked him how he'd know that someone. Surjit said that person would know him.

After getting off the phone with Surjit, Prem phoned Deepa to inform her that he wouldn't be coming over in the afternoon. She wasn't happy. An edge entered her voice when he sidestepped the question about who he was meeting. He could see her revisiting the issue the next time they spoke. He would have to come up with a good story.

He spent the rest of his time at work in a state of expectation, thinking about the man he was meeting, about what he was going to want from him. His eyes frequently zeroed in on his watch to look away with a disappointed shake of the head. Time was hauling itself forward like a bullock cart on a rutted road. If only it would move faster. He couldn't wait to get to the Lodhi Gardens.

When he finally reached, he found the Bara Gumbad deserted. Its scarred façade, topped by the big, gnarled dome, appeared forlorn under the slate-coloured sky. That there was no one about augmented the feeling of desolation. His eyes roved, expecting someone to emerge from the walkways or even out of the ancient monument. When no one did, he settled on a bench to wait. The breeze was cool and there was no sunshine. He had forgotten his sweater at the hotel in his hurry to get to the park on time. He blew on his hands and rubbed them together, wishing he had been more careful. Today was not a day for shirtsleeves.

He was so preoccupied in warming himself that he didn't notice the slim, clean-shaven man with short hair approach the bench. He was surprised when the bench creaked under him as the man sat down. The man's fair skin and sharp features suggested he was Punjabi. Prem eyed him expectantly. The man, on the other hand, failed to acknowledge him. A book emerged in his hands and he began reading without as much as a glance at Prem.

Moments lumbered past. From time to time, Prem would look at the man who only seemed to have eyes for his book. As the silence stretched, Prem became convinced that this man had no interest in him. He wondered whether he should leave. There was no one else in sight and he was freezing.

'So you are Prem,' the man said suddenly.

Prem started. He hadn't expected that.

'Don't look at me,' the man hissed as Prem turned towards him. Prem yanked his eyes away to direct his gaze at the grassy patch in front of the bench.

'You don't know who might be here. We have enemies everywhere. So never look. In fact, you should have brought something to read,' the man said.

'I–I had no idea,' Prem mumbled.

The man muttered something under his breath that Prem could not catch.

'So you want to be part of us,' he said. 'Why? Because you were beaten up?'

Did he want to become a militant because he had been beaten up? That was certainly part of it. But it wasn't all.

'Yes, I was beaten up,' he said. 'And just about every night I have nightmares about it. I would like nothing more than to make the people who beat me up pay, and pay dearly. But that's not why I want to join you. There are other ways for me to make them pay. I don't have to become a militant for that.'

He paused. 'Those riots were organized by people in the government,' he said. 'They were aided and abetted by the police. And then there were the people of Delhi. The Sikhs being butchered were their friends and neighbours. Yet most of them did nothing. Some actually cheered, thinking the Sikhs were getting a well-deserved kick in the pants. The riots would not have been possible without their complicity. How many goondas were there? A few thousand? This is a city of several million.

'They deserve to pay for what happened—all of them—those who organized the riots, those who carried out their orders, and those who stood by and watched it all happen. Otherwise, it will happen again and again.'

His voice grew passionate as he spoke. He ended with his head jerking forward as if to place an exclamation mark at the end of his monologue. The man's face did not change. He merely turned the page of his book, giving little indication that anything Prem had said had registered on him. Seconds dragged past. As the silence grew, so did the uneasiness inside Prem. He wondered where this conversation was headed.

'Before we accept you as one of us, we have to be able to trust you,' the man said finally. 'For that you will have to do something for us.'

'What do you want me to do?' Prem asked.

'Deliver a package.'

* * *

The package was waiting for him at the Oberoi's reception desk the next morning. He collected it during one of his breaks from work and carried it to the gents' bathroom. There, he locked himself inside a stall before unwrapping the shiny pink paper that covered the outside of the box. There was a transistor radio inside.

He ran his fingers over the black surface of the radio. He was supposed to drop it off on a bus right after work.

* * *

The impending delivery had enveloped his mind since leaving the Lodhi Gardens yesterday. It made him anxious and fearful. It also excited him. The thought that he was about to give back as good as he had got, maybe even better, pleased him. He was now part of something bigger and more important than himself; the idea filled him with a sense of purpose he had never known before.

In the midst all of that, a voice was urging him to step back. But it was too weak to change his mind.

He was so caught up in the impending delivery that he forgot all about calling Deepa. By the time he remembered, it was late at night. He made up his mind to call her after making the delivery. She had been perturbed when he told her he wasn't going to be able to come over that day. On top of that, he had forgotten to call, which was sure to piss her off further. She would hurl all kinds of questions and accusations at him. He was in no mood to deal with any of that right now. It was better if he spoke to her after delivering the package.

He was tempted to take the day off from work; the whole idea of waiting tables was repugnant, given what he was going to do later. The man he had met at the Lodhi Gardens, however, warned him against something like that. He'd muttered something incomprehensible under his breath when Prem mentioned his intention to call in sick. 'Are you stupid?' he'd snapped. 'Don't you know breaking a routine attracts attention?' The key to success was to attract as little attention as possible, which meant going to work as usual in the morning.

His excitement had kept him up all night. He was listless and bleary-eyed while serving breakfast. He kept forgetting orders, and delivering others to the wrong tables. He had to be reminded to fill empty glasses and cups. As the afternoon approached, he grew fidgety as well. He dropped plates and spilled tea on the tablecloth, receiving a reprimand from his boss.

At long last, the shift was over. The radio was supposed to be on the 2:10 bus. That didn't leave much time to change, for it would take him a few minutes to get to the bus stop. He practically ran out of the Oberoi in his waiter's uniform.

The bus had arrived by the time he reached the bus stop. It was more than three-fourths full. By the time it pulled out, it was packed. He was glad he had been near the front of the queue to get on.

His heart was hammering in his chest. His mouth was dry and clammy sweat beaded his face. His fingers quivered as he reached inside the box. He willed them to stay still, before turning the radio's knob to *On*. Then he bent down to place the box on the floor. As he straightened, he began to count under his breath, 'One, two, three…'

At the count of ten, the bus came to a stop. He moved towards the exit.

'*Bhaisahib, aap ka box,*' a voice said behind him.

The knots in his stomach tightened. He had to get off the bus. Quickly.

'*Aap ka box, bhaisahib.*'

His face shone with panic. He bumped the man in front of him in his haste. The man swore.

'PREM.'

He froze as Deepa's voice rang out with the resonance of a thunderclap. It couldn't be. He swung around, wide-eyed, to see her standing a few feet away.

He had to get her off the bus. He cried out just as the bomb exploded. He saw Deepa's eyes widen as she careened backwards. As she vanished from sight, the floor fell away from under his feet and he felt himself take to the air. He shot through the roof that had been blown off. His eyes squeezed shut. His body felt like it was on fire. He opened his mouth to scream but no sound came out. Deepa. Where was Deepa? And then he could think no more as the fire engulfed him.

Jaswant smiled upon hearing Savitri's voice on the phone. 'It's Mummy,' he told Rakesh who was sitting across the table from him. Rakesh had stayed back in school that day to watch a football match. After the match, he had come to Jaswant's office, which was close by. He was supposed to spend the rest of the afternoon there before going home with Jaswant. He had just arrived when Savitri called.

Savitri's words were tumbling out at a frenzied pace. Her voice kept getting incoherent as her tears overwhelmed her. The smile on Jaswant's face disappeared as he made out what she was saying. 'You stay where you are, Savitri,' he said. 'I'm coming.'

He jumped out of his chair.

'What happened, Daddy?' Rakesh asked.

Jaswant started. He had forgotten all about Rakesh.

'You stay here,' he said. 'I have to go to Mummy and Didi.'

'What happened, Daddy?'

'I'll tell you later. I have to go now.'

'But Daddy...'

'I *said* I have to go now, Rakesh.'

Jaswant's chin was quivering. His hands kept clenching and unclenching. Sweat dampened his forehead… Rakesh had never seen him in such a state.

'I'm coming with you,' he said.

'*Rakesh.*'

'Otherwise I won't let you go.'

Jaswant didn't want to take Rakesh with him. But more than that, he didn't want to waste time standing about and arguing. 'Okay,' he said finally.

They were on their way in the next few minutes. Rakesh fired question after question at Jaswant. Why had Savitri called? Why were they going to the Oberoi? What was this all about…? Jaswant was evasive. He'd share everything in good time, he told Rakesh. His eyes were glued to the road. Hardly a moment passed without him urging the driver to go faster. His reluctance to answer only piqued Rakesh's curiosity, sparking more questions. What were Savitri and Deepa doing at the Oberoi at this hour? Had they gone there to see Prem…?

They hadn't been on the road for ten minutes before they ran into a police barricade. Jaswant, muttering under his breath, rolled down his window to speak to the inspector in charge.

'Inspector, I have some urgent sarkari work. Let us through immediately.'

'You will have to go round, sir,' the inspector said.

'*Inspector*, I…'

'A bus blew up here, sir.'

Jaswant's mouth hung open as he stared at the inspector. It couldn't be the bus Savitri had told him about; this place was miles from the Oberoi. That meant more than one bus had blown up in Delhi that day. This was starting to look like a well-coordinated militant strike. He told the driver to turn the car round in a hushed voice.

A shocked Rakesh slumped next to him. The news about the bus blowing up had silenced him. Swallowing hard, he glanced at Jaswant. Jaswant stared straight ahead, his face growing grimmer by the minute. On the way they found another road that was closed because a bus had blown up there. Jaswant's worst fears were confirmed. This was indeed a militant strike.

Finally, they were at the Oberoi. The road in front of the hotel was closed. They left the car on the side of the road and ran to the police barricade. Savitri was there with the inspector in charge.

She was pleading with him to let her through the police cordon. Upon seeing them, she started sobbing. Jaswant took her in his arms. She sobbed with her head on his shoulder. Rakesh, who had never seen his parents so disturbed, watched wide-eyed. It was obvious that something terrible had happened. Where was Deepa? His eyes grew frantic at the thought, darting everywhere in vain.

Finally, Savitri was calm enough to speak. Her eyes continued to gleam with tears and, every so often, she was forced to stop and wipe them. Jaswant placed his arm round her shoulders and told her to take her time, it was okay.

She had parked the car at the Oberoi and come out to find Deepa, but had only caught a glimpse of her in the crowd at the bus stop. By the time she got there, Deepa was already on the bus. So she had gone into the Oberoi, thinking she'd phone Jaswant from the lobby to tell him what had happened. No sooner had she entered the lobby than an explosion shook the place. She immediately asked a porter what had happened. He had no idea. People in the lobby were standing about, looking bemused. She ran outside and asked the doorman, who did not know either. Finally, she went out into the street to find people running everywhere. It was several seconds before she could get someone to stop long enough to tell her. A bus had exploded down the street. No sooner had she heard that than the thought it could be the bus Deepa boarded froze her.

She paused, swallowing hard. Jaswant tapped her encouragingly on the shoulder. A little later, she resumed in a wavering voice, 'I ran all the way there. Flames were leaping at the sky. There was smoke everywhere. The police had arrived and were telling everyone to leave. I begged the inspector to let me go through. "My daughter could be on that bus," I told him. But he was adamant. In the end, I asked him to at least let me know the bus's route number. He wasn't sure but then one of the constables...'

Her voice collapsed as she buried her head in Jaswant's coat. Rakesh stood still, unable to believe all this was actually happening. On the other side of the police barricade, he could make out a stretch of open road that led to the scene of the explosion. Before he knew it, his legs had run away with him and he was hurtling in that direction. He didn't get far. A lathi cracked on his back, causing him to cry out. Rough hands grabbed him by the stomach and shoulders. Screaming, he fell to the ground.

Jaswant left Savitri and hurried to the men holding Rakesh. 'Let him go,' he shouted. 'He is my son.'

He brandished his identity card. The inspector's face blanched as he noted that Jaswant was a senior bureaucrat. He immediately instructed his men to release Rakesh.

'My daughter was on that bus, inspector,' Jaswant said. 'My wife has been standing here for ages trying to get news of her. I demand that you let us through.'

'I–I'm sorry, Chopra sahib. But I have my orders. Bombs have gone off in twelve buses all over the city.'

'I don't give a damn about your orders. I want to speak to your superior.'

The inspector started to say something, then apparently thought better of it and spoke into his walkie-talkie before handing it to Jaswant. Jaswant talked to his superior, explaining who he was and the situation they were in. For good measure, he dropped the names of senior police officers that he knew well. Then he handed the walkie-talkie to the inspector, who stood at attention, repeating, 'Yes, sir,' a few times before signing off.

Jaswant told Savitri and Rakesh that the superintendent was sending a jeep over for him. They wouldn't hear of him going alone. The inspector, clearly anxious to put the matter behind him, agreed to let them come as well.

Jaswant and Savitri sat with the driver in the front of the jeep. Rakesh climbed in the back. No one said a word. The jeep's engine was a monotonous backbeat to the dread swamping them. Savitri prayed, clutching Jaswant's hand. Jaswant stared in front of him. Rakesh sat glassy-eyed, unmindful of the jolting jeep or the pain in his back.

The black carcass of the bus emerged. The sky above it was shadowed in smoke. There were ambulances and police vehicles. Medical orderlies bustled about with stretchers. Ambulance sirens wailed. Voices barked orders. The sight of corpses covered with white sheets and lined up on the ground sent a chill through everyone in the jeep.

A deputy superintendent was waiting for them. He shook hands with Jaswant before turning them over to a haggard-looking paramedic, a man with grimy hands and red streaks all over his clothes.

'We have removed some dead bodies to the morgue,' the paramedic said in a tired voice. 'But most of them are still here. You can take a look. I must warn you, though, many of them are badly burnt.'

'What about the survivors?' Jaswant asked.

'We have moved them to the nearest hospital.'

'Can't we see them first?'

'You are looking for your daughter?'

'Yes.'

The paramedic looked down for an instant. 'I'm sorry,' he said, 'but all three survivors are men.'

They pulled Deepa out from under the bodies piled up on what was left of the floor of the bus. Her jaw was gone, as was one side of her face. Her one remaining eye was open, with the pupil dilated; she had died surprised. There were no teeth in what was left of her mouth. Her clothes stuck to her in bits and pieces, with bruises showing livid all over her body. A piece of jagged metal protruded from her right side. She was burnt sooty black.

Prem was lying on the road right next to the scorched shell of the bus. He had hit the ground hard, breaking several bones. His back was badly bruised. Every inch of his face and body had been incinerated.

No one could tell exactly how it happened, not even the survivors. Their memories were hazy, many wiped out by shock. One man said that a young man suddenly started yelling. Another mentioned something about hearing a man screaming at a girl to get off the bus. Suddenly, pandemonium ensued as people began to shout and jostle. That was followed by a deafening explosion.

That was the last any of the survivors recalled. There were explosions in eleven other buses in the city, all around the same time, leading to the conclusion that they had been choreographed. When the police investigated, they discovered that the bomb was lodged inside a transistor radio in each instance.

* * *

Jaswant and Savitri were convinced of Prem's guilt even before the police confirmed it. He had practically run out of the Oberoi, still dressed in his waiter's uniform, to charge onto that bus. Normally, he didn't use buses. Moreover, he had his father's car. Given his involvement with the militants, there could be only one explanation for his behaviour; he was looking to plant a bomb.

Savitri, drowning in grief, ranted against him. That she had championed him as her son-in-law only sharpened her anger. When Amarjeet phoned, she clamoured to give him a piece of her mind. Jaswant prevented her, telling the maid who answered the phone to inform Amarjeet that no one was home. After two more phone calls received the same response, Amarjeet got the message and stopped ringing.

* * *

As the days passed, Savitri's resentment against Prem was overtaken by the guilt she felt for making the rishta happen. 'None of this would have happened if I had listened to you,' she told Jaswant, her voice tearing out of her like a lament. He tried to comfort her the best he could. But there was only so much he could do; he had his own grief to grapple with.

Savitri insisted on keeping Deepa's room exactly as it was when Deepa was alive. She made sure the bed was made every morning. In the evening, the covers were pulled back, making the bed look like it was waiting for Deepa to settle in for the night. Deepa's dresses continued to hang in the almirah. Every couple of days, Savitri would get one of them washed and ironed as if Deepa had just worn it. Deepa's books remained in the bookcase, as did her records scattered on top of it. From time to time, Savitri would open one of her old notebooks and spend hours studying Deepa's scrawl. Or she'd play one of Deepa's records on the stereo. When Rakesh first heard 'Take a chance on me' filling the house, he wondered if Deepa had come back from the dead. Upon going to Deepa's room, he was taken aback to find Savitri there. His mother playing an Abba record! It was years before he realized that Savitri was actually playing Deepa.

* * *

Jaswant, in the meanwhile, was going through his own self-flagellation. That his doubts about the match had been well-founded did not make him feel any better. Rather, it made him kick himself even more for consenting to the marriage. Instead of trusting his good sense, he had allowed himself to be swayed by his wife and daughter. Deepa was young and foolish. Savitri had not been ravaged by Partition. They could be excused for their naiveté. He, on other hand, had experienced the worst of Partition and knew first-hand what could happen when hate drove all love and compassion from people's hearts. Yet he had allowed himself to be swayed. If he had been firmer, none of this would have happened and Deepa would still be alive.

Outwardly, he strove to give little hint of the storm raging inside him. He was, after all, the man of the house. He had to be strong for everyone. If he lost it, then what would become of the others? Yet there were times when the weight of the clouds brooding inside him became too hard to carry; when he was forced to retreat to his room or bathroom, any place where he could be alone, to allow the grief welling inside him to flow.

Jaswant and Savitri attempted to comfort Rakesh the best they could. But the effort was too much. Their own pain proved far too debilitating for them to offer any kind of lasting comfort. Rakesh was left to make sense of things on his own.

Operation Bluestar and Indira Gandhi's assassination had done little to alter his world. The concern for Prem's safety during the riots had ebbed away after his safe return. The sight of gun-toting policemen in the streets and metal detectors outside cinemas had been nothing more than an aggravation. School, sports and friends had hogged his attention, leaving him little time to mull over what was going on. It was Savitri's call to Jaswant's office that had changed everything. In less than a minute, the world had become unreal. The mantra of *this can't be happening* had swamped his thoughts all the way to the Oberoi. The revelation about the bombs exploding in buses had only added to his disbelief. The sight of Deepa's mangled corpse induced a trance-like state that lasted right through the funeral, the chautha, the terevi, the immersion of the ashes in the Ganga… Even after the death rituals had been completed, the look of disbelief refused to leave his face.

Until then, death had existed for him in newspapers and movies. He had never seen anyone die. His mates in school would mention the death of grandparents, but that was far removed from his world—his paternal grandparents had died before he was born, while his maternal grandparents were both dead before he was three. Since he had never known them, he did not feel their absence.

Deepa's demise changed all that by stripping death off its otherworldliness and planting it firmly in his life. Everywhere he looked, it was staring him in the face: in the stricken look that never left his mother; in his father's long silences. More than anything, it was there in Deepa's absence that robbed his world of its vitality.

As his disbelief ebbed away, the tears frozen inside him came to life. Purging himself of his tears, however, did nothing to purge the feeling of desolation that would strike without warning to leave him disconsolate. The sight of fire reminded him of Deepa. It didn't matter whether it sprang from a choolah or a cigarette lighter, or the sacred fire binding a couple in holy matrimony. The nauseating stench of burning flesh would invade his nose and mouth, causing his stomach to lurch as he envisioned the blaze working its way through Deepa—inch by inch, body part by body part— until she was burnt the colour of soot.

It was after such moments that he found himself

thinking of Seema. Regret and embarrassment seemed to be waiting to swamp him whenever his thoughts turned to her. Not for a moment had he stopped to consider what she was going through in the days following Indira Gandhi's assassination, not even after she let slip the fact that the Kohlis were getting calls from land sharks interested in procuring their property. Even before any one of them could speak, they would ask, 'When are you leaving?' She had told him that in a low voice before turning a quizzical face to him. Evidently, she expected a reaction. All he could manage was an uncomprehending look before moving on to something else. What had made his behaviour worse was that she wasn't the only person he knew whose life was being distorted. About two weeks after the riots, his Sikh friend Gurcharan's parents had pulled him out of school. They were moving to Amritsar. *We are going to live among our own people*, was how Gurcharan explained the move— Gurcharan, who was born and bred in Delhi. A little later, a Sikh classmate, Harjinder, had mentioned that she and her family, who had just moved to Delhi, were being forced to live at her uncle's because no one in Delhi would rent their house to a Sikh… He had listened to both of them, as he had to Seema, without registering a word. It needed his own tragedy to pull him out of his apathy.

He understood that the break with the Kohlis

was inevitable, given what had happened. But that didn't stop him from wanting to tell Seema that he was sorry for the way he had acted and explaining that he finally understood… After mulling it over for a few days, he made up his mind to call her. He realized that she might not want to talk to him, but he had to make the effort. If her father or mother answered, he was prepared to hang up.

He called from a public phone. A recording informed him that the Kohlis' phone had been disconnected.

That was the last thing he had expected. He phoned again, thinking there might be a mistake, to get the same recording. He spent the rest of the day wondering what could have happened. He couldn't think of an explanation that made sense. Surely the Kohlis would have paid their telephone bill on time.

The next morning, he got off his school bus on the way to school. In a public bathroom, he changed from his school uniform into a spare set of clothes that he'd carried along. Then he took an autorickshaw to Seema's school, where he pretended to be her cousin who had come with a message from her father.

Her class teacher informed him that Seema hadn't come to school in days.

He was nonplussed. He decided to go to her house. When he reached the house, he found the front gate locked. The boundary wall was a mess of hate graffiti calling the Kohlis all kinds of names. All the windows in the house that faced the street were boarded up. The cars, though, were parked in the driveway which meant everyone was home. He searched for the bell. There had been one right next to the front gate. It was nowhere to be found.

Finally, he called out her name. There was no answer. After calling several times to no avail, he left.

'If you'd only listened to me, our boy would still be alive and we'd be far away from this hellhole. But you wouldn't, would *you*? All you could think of was yourself. Now look what's happened.' Kishneet's grief and anger surged out of her in frenetic rants that suddenly broke off to leave her face teary and crumpled. Amarjeet listened in silence, the pain in his face etching deeper with each reproach.

It wasn't Kishneet's ranting that haunted him as much as the belief that he hadn't done his duty by his son. All Kishneet's words did was reiterate what he had come to believe all the way from his core. Prem had been beaten badly. The beating he had received was sure to have inflicted wounds that went far more than skin-deep, engendering a seething residue of anger and resentment. In such a frame of mind, he was bound to be susceptible to militant rhetoric. Yet he, Prem's father, who should have protected him from all that, had left him to his own devices once his physical injuries healed. Rather than do what he had to in order to save his son, he had focused on saving his home!

That thought cut him up like nothing else. The

hopes he had pinned on Prem. All those years spent transforming himself from a penniless refugee to an eminent doctor—slaving through a rotting government school, studying under street lights because there was never any electricity in his shabby house, working odd jobs to get through the medical degree... A lifetime of slights and sacrifices seemed worth it the moment he looked at Prem; Prem, who was an MBA and had gone to one of the city's best private schools; Prem, who was engaged to a senior bureaucrat's daughter; Prem, who never had to enter any place through the back door... His heart would flood with gladness each time he contemplated the future awaiting his son.

Now Prem was dead, thanks to his negligence.

His guilt announced itself all over him. It was there in his sagging shoulders; in the new lines on his face that made him appear twenty years older; in his shambling gait and worn clothes... It pulled him away from work, shutting him up in the house day and night. It chased away his sleep and killed his appetite for food or conversation. It turned him into a man who appeared to have no truck with the world, a man who sweated it out alone with his demons.

Sometimes during his musings, the face of the woman Jaswant and he had encountered while bringing Prem home from Trilokpuri would appear from nowhere. She was no longer beseeching him to save her son. She was watching him with a smirk on her face.

* * *

One morning, he had just emerged from a restless night and was sitting in bed in his kurta-pyjama when Kishneet came to tell him that Seema was refusing to go to school.

His senses were dull and he gazed at her blankly. Only after she repeated herself did her words register. A frown unfurled itself across his forehead as he heaved himself out of bed. Just the day before, Seema had gone back to school for the first time after Prem's death. Upon returning in the afternoon, she had headed straight to her room to stay there the rest of the day. She hadn't said anything to him or Kishneet.

His legs felt just as weary as they had the night before as he followed Kishneet to the drawing room in his rubber slippers. Seema was slumped on the sofa in her nightgown. Her ragged hair fell loosely on her shoulders while her eyes gazed at nothing in particular.

'What is this I hear from your mother?' he said. 'Why don't you want to go to school?'

Seema didn't look at him. He repeated his question. She continued to look away, clenching her lips so tightly that her face appeared pinched.

'What is it, Seema?' Amarjeet persisted.

There was a short pause before Seema said, 'It's all so horrible.'

Her voice was low, practically a whisper. Amarjeet glanced at Kishneet who shrugged her shoulders to indicate she was just as clueless.

'What is so horrible?' he asked.

'Everything,' Seema said. 'The minute I step out of the house people stare and point fingers. "*Khooni ki bahen, khooni ki bahen*," someone cries out. They practically shout it out to the entire neighbourhood. Even in the car to school...I can't handle it. Yesterday they told me they don't want me there with them. People have been calling them ugarwadi for days. But I guess being called a terrorist is not as bad as being associated with a *khooni ki bahen*. At school no one speaks to me. Not even my friends since nursery school. Yesterday they were all taken aback to see me there. Even the teachers were looking at me as if they had seen a ghost.'

Her voice broke as she finished. Amarjeet swallowed. He should have expected something like this after what had happened. But he had been so wrapped up in his grieving.

'Go to your room,' he told Seema.

She rose, wiping her eyes with her hands. After she was gone, Kishneet demanded, 'You still want to stay here?'

He didn't answer.

* * *

He remained hunched in a chair in the drawing room after Kishneet left to be with Seema. The bell at the front gate rang to jolt him out of his brooding. He had no wish to go outside, but there was no one else to attend to the bell. Vishnu had gone to the Mother Dairy depot to get milk. He got up and went out to see two loutish men with thick oily hair at the gate. Upon seeing him, they began to yell. '*Desh drohi, ugarwadi, khooni…*' Maybe it was what they were yelling or maybe it emanated from what Seema had recounted to him earlier. His anger swelled and, before he knew it, he was shouting, 'Shut up, you bastards.' Far too incensed to give a damn, he charged at them with his arm raised. Perhaps it was the naked intent in his eyes, or just that they didn't expect him to come at them like that. They promptly swivelled around and ran for their lives.

Still fuming, Amarjeet opened the gate and went out. He had made up his mind to rip out the bell. The black graffiti scrawled all over the boundary wall made him pause. He decided to deal with the bell later. The first thing to do was call a security agency. They needed a twenty-four-hour guard to take care of such hooligans.

One of his patients, Brigadier Suri, had opened a security firm after retiring from the army. Amarjeet found his card in his wallet and phoned the brigadier who picked up at the third ring. Quickly, Amarjeet told him what he wanted. There was a pause, before the brigadier said, 'I'm sorry, Amarjeet, but I can't do it. After what has happened, I can't allow my firm to be associated with you. Our reputation will be mud in no time.'

Three weeks after his futile visit to Seema's home, Rakesh ran into her in Connaught Place. He had gone there with some friends after school. They had just finished lunch at Nirula's and were in the process of leaving when he spotted her in the verandah outside the restaurant.

He had spent the past three weeks racking his brains for a way to get to her. He kept phoning in the vain hope that her phone would be reconnected. He flirted with the idea of writing, only to find himself incapable of finding the right words. In the end, he decided what he had to say could not be written down. If they'd had a mutual friend, he could have sent her a message. But they did not.

To have her suddenly materialize outside the restaurant's glass door was like a revelation—and an opportunity he did not want to miss. He excused himself from his friends and ran out of the restaurant with his satchel of books bouncing on his back. Once he was outside, he called out her name at the top of his voice.

He was taken aback when she turned around. Very little remained of the girl he had known. Her face was thinner and the eyes no longer shone with life. The hair, instead of cascading freely down her shoulders, was trapped at the back of her head in a tight bun. But, more than anything, everything about her appeared spent; the faded blue jeans and red T-shirt she had on; the legs that seemed to haul her forward; the lines on her face... In the years to come, he'd marvel at how foreign her voice sounded, so much older and loaded with bitterness. But, in the moment, it was *what* she said that froze him.

'Why don't you walk past as if I'm a stranger?' It rang out like a taunt, accompanied by a chilling smile. It was the last thing he had expected.

'After all I'm a *khooni ki bahen*,' she continued. 'That's what they call me in my neighbourhood. They shout it out whenever they see me: *Khooni ki bahen, khooni ki bahen*...' He was shocked by what she was saying, but couldn't get himself to speak. She seemed unable to stop, the words spilling out of her. 'It got so bad that I stopped going out altogether. That didn't stop them. They came home and rang the bell at the gate. The moment Daddy would come out, they would scream all kinds of names at him. Daddy got rid of the bell and boarded the windows that face the street. Then they stuffed our mailbox with hate mail. He even had the mailbox removed. They began making anonymous phone calls. Finally, Daddy got the phone disconnected.'

Rakesh had heard stories of such things happening to Sikhs in Delhi. But the Kohlis had lived in Shanti Niketan for years. Moreover, it was a well-to-do neighbourhood, not some resettlement colony.

A tremor entered her voice as she continued, 'Nobody understands what we are going through,' she said. 'Or, as Mummy says, nobody wants to. I have lost my only brother, Mummy and Daddy their only son. We have lost our friends, our respectability… Now we are even going to lose our home.'

'What?' Rakesh said.

'Yes, we are leaving for Seattle tomorrow. We won't be coming back.'

He stared at her, his face incredulous.

'I guess it's for the better,' she said in a low voice. 'No one knows us there.' Her lips pressed together as her gaze fell. 'I just came out for one last look.'

She appeared so desolate, standing there in those run-down clothes with her eyes and shoulders drooping. He found himself stepping forward to put his arms round her. She clung to him, crying softly with her head resting on his shoulder. He gently stroked her back where her lustrous hair used to flow. He had no idea how long they stood there holding each other. She was the one who finally stepped back to dry her eyes with a handkerchief. He remained where he was.

By now she had recovered her composure. She told him she had to go. He asked her for her address in America. They were going to stay with one of her father's friends for a while, she said, and she didn't know his address off the top of her head. He implored her to write, promising he'd write back. She nodded, but something told him she was merely indulging him. She'd never write.

He watched her walk away from him down the arcade. He thought of calling her back and gave up the thought. There was intent in the stride that was taking her away from him; a finality that he could not reverse. So he stayed where he was, watching her retreating figure with a sickening emptiness swirling inside him,

Just before she melted into the milling crowd, he thought he saw her pause as if she was going to turn around. But then she strode forward and was gone.

Delhi 2004

Just before she melts into the milling crowd, he thinks he sees her pause as if she is going to turn around. But then she strides forward and is gone.

He is now wide awake, lying on his back in bed. The ceiling fan hangs motionless above him. Through the window to his right, he can make out the grey early November morning spreading itself across the sky. He is thinking of the dream he just had; of the scene that repeats itself without fail whenever he thinks of Seema. Like a film reel stuck in a frame, refusing to go backward or forward. He moved on from that time a long time ago. Since then, he has lived, loved, lost…Yet when it comes to Seema, he remains frozen in that moment.

What made him dream of her now, he wonders. He hasn't thought of her in ages. These days, all he can think of is his dead wife Roma. Each day he prays for so much fatigue to crowd into his bones that sleep overcomes him the moment his head touches the pillow. During the day, he has a routine to distract him. At night, he is as defenceless as a knight stripped off his armour. Memories of Roma crowd round him more thickly than ever in the dead of the night, sometimes coming at him like a mob intent on ripping his soul to pieces, even the happy ones laced with despair.

He recognizes Savitri's shuffling gait in the passage outside. Jaswant has more of a plodding footfall. Savitri must have been in Deepa's room. She's probably been up all night thinking of her. Even though it's been twenty years, his parents have not recovered from Deepa's demise. There are times when their smiles radiate genuine joy and their laughter loses its customary hollowness. But those moments never last long.

They spend their lives hovering at the edge of the despair that comes from being sunk in a past that cannot be reclaimed and yet remains too dear to shed. They can spend hours speculating on what Deepa would be like if she had lived. She'd be a mother now. Her first child would have completed school and be well on the way to finishing college. Her second child would be in school. Would she have two boys or two girls or one of each…?

To this day, Savitri refuses to hear of anyone else using her room. When he moved back home after Roma's death, she had insisted he stay in the room he'd had as a boy even though Deepa's room is bigger. 'As long as I'm alive, it will always be hers,' she says. 'When I'm up there with her you can do what you wish.' She continued to play Deepa's records for as long as she could. It was a decade before she agreed to donate Deepa's clothes to charity. Her books and notebooks she retains to this day.

Not much has changed in the house in the last two decades. Unlike all their neighbours, they have not constructed new floors. The colour of the walls remains the same, although they have been re-painted a few times. Some pieces of furniture have been replaced. A few new pictures have gone up, and there is a new TV in the drawing room...But the essential character of the place remains what it was in the eighties. The house is an anachronism in a Delhi transforming beyond belief.

He glances at his watch lying on the side table next to the bed. It is almost time to get up. He climbs out of bed and, thrusting his feet into a pair of rubber slippers, he makes his way to the kitchen for chai. Savitri is already there, making a cup for herself. She tells him that she'll get him one as well. He goes out to collect the newspaper from the front porch. The cool breeze causes him to hurry back in to the drawing room where he settles in an overstuffed chair to read.

There is an article about the '84 riots on the editorial page. Indira Gandhi's assassination had its twentieth anniversary a few days ago. The piece reads like it has been recycled from the one printed last year around the same time. The brutality of the rioters, the ringleaders getting away scot-free, the victims still waiting for justice...These themes get pulled out of mothballs year after year when the anniversary comes round. He continues to be amazed by how everything that happened has shrunk to a few recyclable paragraphs of newsprint.

Savitri keeps him company as he has his chai. Jaswant, who retired nine years ago, prefers to sleep in these days. Her hair is short, going from crow black to steely grey in the last two decades. It remains thick towards the front and middle, before tapering in a V at the nape of her neck. Since 1992, she has been wearing glasses which actually help hide some of the dark pouches under her eyes. Even now, her insomnia, which was endemic in the years following Deepa's death, flares occasionally.

Yesterday she went to a friend's grandson's birthday party. A forlorn look settles on her face as she describes the occasion. He can sense her revisiting her regret over not having a grandchild. He can't think of anything to say that might help. So he keeps quiet.

After finishing his chai, he goes to get ready for office. After a quick breakfast, he leaves. In no time, he and his Maruti Esteem are immersed in the jostle of a typical Delhi morning. To get anywhere in Delhi in 2004 you have to push and shove. If you're driving, you jostle your way through snarling traffic, angry at being choked to death on roads shrunk to half their size by the ongoing construction of the metro. If you're walking, you thrust past pedestrians, dogs, cattle and hawkers of various hues crammed onto dusty, crumbling pavements. If you're using public transport, you heave in and out of buses bulging with humanity… When you're done with the pushing and shoving, the relief that ensues comes tempered by the realization that you have to do it all over again at the end of the day.

That morning the ceaseless jostling takes more out of him than usual and he finds his eyes closing as he waits behind the wheel of his car at a red light. Before he knows it, he is in the Delhi he knew as a boy. The Delhi that nosed its way into the green and shining after the 1982 Asian Games. The Delhi of radiant skies and mornings packed with birdsong and water fountains frolicking in the middle of roundabouts and air heady with the sweetness of saptaparni and raat ki rani.

An angry horn yanks him back to 2004. He holds up his hand to apologize to the driver behind him and concentrates on getting to his office in one piece. He is relieved to find an empty parking slot in front of his office building.

His office, an advertising agency, is on the third floor. He wishes he was wearing a warm suit as he makes his way into the building with his briefcase. Unlike on other days, the chill of the morning hasn't fizzled out, despite the sun's attempts to brighten the sickly pallor of the sky. It appears winter is closing in even though they are still in early November.

The old lift starts moving with a creak to come to a jarring halt on his floor. He steps out. His secretary, Asha, informs him that she has placed the proofs of the Northwest Airlines ad on his desk as he makes his way to his cabin. Inside, he loosens his tie and settles in his revolving chair to open the brown envelope containing the proofs. Immediately, he catches his breath.

Although he hasn't seen her in twenty years, the woman in the picture is unquestionably Seema.

Dressed in a sari, she is smiling with her hands folded in front of her in a namaste. Her hair is different from what he remembers—more brown than black and combed back from the forehead rather than falling forward in a wave. Her skin has lightened to the colour of old ivory (or is that the photographer's lighting?) Her eyes are still dark and luminous, albeit with a suggestion of crow's feet near the edges. And is that a line on one end of her smile? Maybe. All said and done, the years sit well on her. She is every bit as striking as she was at sixteen.

He picks up the phone and calls his secretary. 'Asha, can you get Kishore for me?'

Presently Kishore comes on the line. 'Good morning, sir.' The younger man's concern is palpable. He has probably been up all night wondering whether his boss will like the ad.

'Kishore, I was just looking at the proofs for

the Northwest Airlines ad. The model you've used here, I don't remember her ever working for our agency.'

'She's not a model, sir; she's one of their flight attendants. When we do an ad for a foreign airline, sir, sometimes we use one of their Indian flight attendants. Her name's Seema Kohli, sir. And she was ekdum fantastic. I picked her up for the photo shoot from the Maurya at ten yesterday morning and she was back there by lunchtime, sir.'

Seema Kohli. She still has the same last name. Does that mean she's not married?

'All right, Kishore, good job.'

'Thank you, sir.' The relief in Kishore's voice is just as palpable as his concern a little earlier.

He puts down the phone and sits gazing at Seema's picture. He is still looking at it when Asha calls to let him know that it is time for his morning meeting.

It is an effort to keep his mind on the job right through the meeting. Memories from the eighties drop in like a bunch of infuriating, uninvited guests and he is forced to somehow shut the door in their face.

Relieved that the meeting is finally over, he tells Asha that he is going for a coffee break to the cafe across the street. As he descends in the lift that creaks alarmingly throughout by this time of the day, he thinks of the last time he saw Seema. Now what comes to mind before anything else is her lustrous hair forced in an unremarkable bun. That she had tried so hard to go unnoticed speaks volumes about how overwhelmed she had felt amidst the hate.

If the picture on his desk is anything to go by, she has put all that behind her.

The doors of the lift grind open and he steps out to walk through the lobby. He catches sight of himself in the glass-panelled walls. His shoulders slouch. His hair is thin and greying. There are wrinkles on his forehead. Dark circles hem in his eyes. A paunch protrudes under his coat … No one looking at him will guess he is only thirty-six.

Outside, the sun has been defeated in its efforts to light up the sky. An ashen sky, stricken by a murky haze, greets him. The air is irksome, clutching at his throat while causing his eyes to water. The street he crosses is packed with impatient traffic jostling for every inch of space. It is jarring to emerge in this cluttered universe after spending so much of the morning in the expansiveness of the eighties.

He is relieved when he finally makes it to the other side of the street and enters the cafe. As he waits for his order at the counter, he looks through the glass double doors and large windows at the street running outside. A Congress Party billboard with the likeness of Prime Minister Manmohan Singh greets him from the other side of the road. A Sikh prime minister. Who could have imagined that in 1984…?

A bus slides into view. An old Delhi Transport Corporation bus, painted yellow and green, the kind that was the norm in the eighties. *Deepa burnt sooty black, her clothes sticking to her in bits and pieces, bruises showing livid all over her body, her jaw gone, one eye smashed, the other one wide-open as if in surprise.* Shivers ripple through him. He grips the counter, fearing he might go reeling. The barista eyes him with concern. Her lips move. He has no idea what she is saying. He tries to speak, but the words jam in his throat. Her lips continue to move and this time he makes out a few words, '…seat…bring…

drink…' Yes, thank you, he nods, thank you very much.

He chooses a table where he can sit with his back to the street. At the adjoining table, a man is working on a laptop computer. Three tables away, a woman jabbers into a cellphone. He is in a place that could never have existed in Delhi in 1984, surrounded by things that would have seemed just as unlikely then. Yet he is there staring at a bus…

'Sir,' it is the barista with his latte. She is a young girl in her teens. She wouldn't have existed then either. He thanks her. She lingers, wanting to know if everything is all right. He wonders how she will react if he told her seeing an old bus flung him back two decades. At her age, a blast from the past is an old video on MTV. But he merely smiles and thanks her for her concern, saying he feels fine now.

After she is gone, he sips his coffee slowly. His family is not the only one to be left gutted by what happened in 1984. There are countless others, and many would have lost more. The thought gives him little comfort. Happiness can be shared with others, but misery is a cross you bear on your own.

* * *

He wonders how it has gone for the Kohlis.

The neighbourhood could be in Bellevue, Redmond, Issaquah…any upper-class suburb of Seattle. Yet here it is, spread out in the heart of Delhi. A gated community with private security guards. One of them—a slim, middle-aged man with an erect military bearing—stops Seema's taxi at the gate and asks her where she is going. When she tells him that she has come to visit her cousin Daman, he calls Daman on his cellphone to confirm. Only then does he let the taxi through.

As they drive deeper into the neighbourhood, the resemblance to America becomes even stronger. There are neat rows of brownstone houses, unseparated by fences or boundary walls, with plush green gardens at the front and back, and compacts and SUVs parked in the driveway. In one of the gardens, a sprinkler is spraying water. Seema gazes wide-eyed at that. Until now, she has not seen a sprinkler in India. Certainly there wasn't one in 1984.

Manpreet, her six-year-old daughter, is just as wide-eyed. Her surprise is different; she is pleasantly overcome after running into something familiar in a foreign country. Her little face, with its eager eyes and mop of curly black hair, contemplates the leaping water with a brilliant smile.

'*Woh hai number 45,*' the driver says.

He points to one of the houses. The taxi eases to a stop in front of it. Seema pays the driver and alights with her daughter. Taking the little girl's hand, she walks up to the front door and rings the doorbell. A servant girl, in her mid-teens, answers. Seeing her is oddly reassuring. A servant, a girl in a cheap salwar-kameez, who speaks no English, underlines the fact that this is still India.

Seema and Manpreet follow the girl to the drawing room. Seema can see just how much Daman has moved up in the world as she walks through the hallway. Back in the eighties, Daman and her family were poor relatives crowding into a tiny DDA flat in Karol Bagh. Now Daman owns a spacious home in a tony neighbourhood. The well-polished marble floor is a far cry from the rough cement flooring in the old DDA flat. An M.F. Husain painting occupies pride of place on one wall. The drawing room contains a Persian carpet, crystal vases, designer furniture... In the last two decades Daman has gone from being the impoverished daughter of a struggling government clerk to the wife of a rich investment banker who vacations in Singapore and Bangkok.

While Daman's star has risen, Seema and her

family have been scraping and saving to establish themselves in America. Merely securing a foothold took years. In his haste to spirit them away from a hostile Delhi, Amarjeet sold everything off at throwaway prices. When they arrived in Seattle, they did not have enough to start over. Amarjeet's Indian degree made him ineligible to practise in America. He was forced to swallow his pride and take a personal loan from the friend in whose home they stayed during their first year in Seattle, and open a convenience store. For years, it seemed as if they were living on a piece of flotsam that might sink at any minute. They moved constantly, each time to a more modest apartment. Making the rent was a perpetual concern. Many times they were late, and not all apartment managers were understanding; they brandished eviction orders, forcing Amarjeet to beg for extensions. There were nights where Seema lay awake, wondering whether they'd still have a roof over their heads the next morning.

The fragility of such an existence made her go to a junior college after finishing high school. It was far more economical than the university. Their fortunes began to mend only after she finished junior college and started working as a flight attendant. Her decision gutted Amarjeet, who had his heart set on making her a doctor. 'Do you know what you are doing?' he demanded. 'You are a doctor's daughter. How can you even *think* of becoming a glorified ayah?'

Even now she can remember the look of defeat settling on his face when he realized he could not change her mind. He was thinking that he had failed her, which for him was a double whammy because he already believed he had failed Prem. She hated herself for bringing him to such a pass. But she had no choice. The burden of being the sole breadwinner was killing him. He was racked by constant backache and had begun to stoop while walking. She couldn't see him go on like that any longer.

Her going to work meant they were able to buy their own home within two years. For her, that house is more precious than any palace. It makes the memory of their difficult years in America bearable. But it is an ordinary home in a middle-class American neighbourhood. There is no way it can match the opulence of Daman's house. In the eighties, a smug Kishneet would mouth, '*Ji sab kismet da khel hai*,' to sum up the difference in social status between her family and Daman's. Now Daman can employ the same smugness to make a similar pronouncement about them.

* * *

Pursing her lips, she enters the drawing room with Manpreet. It is twice the size of her drawing room in America. Daman is sitting in the sofa with a tall, bearded man with shoulder-length black hair. In the eighties, she was a dusky, slender girl who wore hand-me-downs. Now she is a plump woman, with fair, almost yellow skin, dressed in an unwrinkled designer kurta-pyjama. Her unsullied kurta makes Seema conscious of how creased and faded her shirt and Manpreet's frock are. In Seattle, where no one irons their clothes, it is fine. In India, where press-wallahs abound at every street corner, it is not proper.

Daman introduces the man as Manjit Grewal. 'Manjit and my husband grew up together in Chandigarh,' she tells Seema. 'Manjit is a journalist with *Hindustan Times*.'

Turning to Manjit, she adds, 'This is my cousin sister Seema and her daughter Manpreet. They are here from Seattle. Seema is the model in the family.'

'I'm no model,' Seema says, laughing.

'Nonsense,' Daman says. 'When you are in an ad you are a model.'

'Seattle?' Manjit mouths. 'Then you must work for Microsoft or Boeing.'

'Not every Indian in Seattle works for Microsoft or Boeing,' Seema tells him. 'I'm a flight attendant with Northwest Airlines.'

Daman tells the servant girl to get chai. Manjit starts quizzing her about Seattle. For him the city is all about Bill Gates, Nirvana and *Sleepless in*

Seattle—all of which is a world away from what she knows. She answers the best she can. When she is done with her chai, she says, 'We should be going.'

'Arre, come on, have some more chai,' Daman says.

'No, we should go. I promised to take Manpreet to Shanti Niketan and show her where we used to live. We have to be at the airport by eight this evening. It's already past twelve. We should get going.'

'I can give you a ride to Shanti Niketan,' Manjit tells her.

'Oh, no, please don't bother, we'll get...'

'It's no bother. I have to leave anyway. I have an important interview coming up and Shanti Niketan is right on my way. Please, I insist.'

It would be impolite to say no to him. 'Okay, thank you very much,' she says, smiling.

He asks them to wait for him while he gets his car, parked in one of the side streets. There is a sly smile on Daman's face, which makes Seema wonder if there is more to this than Manjit simply being helpful. She'll find out soon enough.

Daman wraps a shawl round herself to accompany them outside. As Manpreet skips ahead, Daman says in a low voice, 'I think he likes you. I've never seen him so keen to give anyone a ride before. What's more, he's divorced as well, with no children.'

Seema wants to shake her head in disbelief. Daman probably set it all up, calling Manjit at the same time she was going to visit. India hasn't changed that much in the last twenty years; divorcees are still supposed to marry each other.

Daman wraps the shawl even more tightly round herself as they come out of the house. 'God, it's chilly,' she says. 'Aren't you cold in that thin shirt? I can understand Manpreet not feeling cold. She was born and raised there. But you are from here.'

'But I've been living there for the last twenty years.'

'I can see that,' Daman's gaze travels over the wrinkles in Seema's shirt. Seema pretends not to notice, concentrating on Manpreet who is taken with the dahlias in the garden. When Manjit's car arrives, she says goodbye to Daman. After making sure that Manpreet is safely secured in the back of the car, she climbs into the seat next to Manjit. Soon they are off.

'This place looks just like America, doesn't it?' Manjit says.

'Yeah, I can't believe it's in Delhi. Delhi seems to have changed so much. The Delhi I remember was all Punjabi. But ever since I've come here, I've been running into Biharis, Oriyas, South Indians... I've seen people shopping in malls, watching movies in multiplexes. Now I see a neighbourhood like this one.'

'Yes, we have grown,' Manjit says. 'And now we have the malls and the multiplexes, the nightclubs and the five-star hotels.' He pauses as they hit a bump on a section of the road that is unpaved. 'And we still have the kachcha roads and the jhuggis, the power cuts and the poor water supply. So don't be fooled by everything you see.' Turning to her, he asks, 'When did you leave India?'

'1984.'

His face tightens in a grimace. 'I can imagine how bad it would have been then. Even when I came here in '91 things were bad. Everyone called us ugarwadi. It was hard to get a place to rent. For six months, I stayed with my uncle because no one wanted to rent a place to a Sikh. Finally, I cut my hair and shaved off my beard. I didn't tell anyone I was a Sikh. Even then, I got a place only because my landlord was a South Indian who had no idea that Grewal is a Sikh name... Nowadays, they talk only of Mrs Gandhi's assassination. But so much more was assassinated—amity built up over generations, friendship, trust, decency...' He fingers his beard as he adds, 'Now we are the good guys all over again.'

Seema glances over her shoulder at Manpreet. She is relieved to find her paying no attention to the conversation; she is staring wide-eyed at a cow on the pavement. Manpreet knows nothing about what happened in '84.

It takes them another twenty minutes to reach Shanti Niketan. Manjit does most of the talking. He tells her about his job and the impossible hours it demands. Which is why he is thinking of giving it up and becoming an editor. At least then he'll be able to work regular hours. He circles to his past, talking about growing up in Chandigarh and adjusting to life in the big city… She listens politely. She senses his curiosity in the way he often pauses to glance at her. He wants to get to know her better. By telling her about himself, he is hoping that she'll reply in kind. She does not. He seems nice enough, but she can't see herself with him.

At Shanti Niketan, he asks if she wants a ride to the airport in the evening. She shakes her head, telling him she already has one.

* * *

It takes her a while to find the old house. The houses in Shanti Niketan look so foreign that she finds herself going about in circles. When she does, she can barely recognize it. Now it has a kiosk outside, where a uniformed security guard sits in attendance. The boundary wall is higher. A large tree looms in the garden. From what she can make out through the tree's thick branches, the building behind it is not a house any longer. There are three grey-coloured apartments constructed one on top of the other. A glance at the nameplate next to the gate confirms as much; three families live in that compound.

'That's it,' she tells Manpreet.

Manpreet gazes in the direction of her pointing finger. 'I can't see anything,' she says.

Seema lifts her up so that she can look through the tree's branches. 'It's very different now,' she says. 'We had no security kiosk. The gate too was painted black. That tree wasn't there in the garden and the structure wasn't grey but light yellow. And it was a house then not an apartment building.'

'Hello.' It is the security guard from inside the kiosk.

Seema puts Manpreet down. She doesn't like the rough tone the man employed. She wonders what made him address them in that manner. They are merely standing in front of the house. Then she remembers how faded and creased their clothes are. She sets her lips in a tight line.

'Yes, what's the matter?' she demands in English.

The man's face blanches. He comes out of the kiosk. He is a wiry, middle-aged man, dressed in a light blue shirt and navy-blue trousers.

'So sorry, ma'am,' he says in Hindi, 'but we get so many loafers here. We have to be careful. If you can tell me who you want to meet, I can call them and let you in.'

'Oh, no,' Seema says, speaking Hindi now. 'We have come from America. This used to be our home when we lived in India. I just wanted to show my daughter where it was. She's come to India for the first time.'

The man's forehead furrows as he examines her face. 'I've been here since 1990 but I don't remember you,' he says.

'We were here well before that,' she tells him.

The furrows deepen on the man's forehead. 'When I began working here, I heard a Sikh family lived here in the eighties. They left for America. I believe their son…'

'That wasn't us,' she interrupts.

She is glad they are speaking in Hindi which Manpreet cannot follow. Manpreet has been told that Prem died in an accident.

'Let's go,' she says to Manpreet, 'it's almost time for lunch.'

'Can't we go in?' Manpreet asks.

'No, we can't. We'd be trespassing.'

She nods to the security guard who folds his hands in a namaste before turning to go back inside his kiosk.

'What was he saying about Sikhs and America?' Manpreet asks as they walk away.

'Oh, he made a mistake. He thought we were someone else. So what would you like for lunch?' She is keen to change the subject as soon as possible. The ruse works as Manpreet realizes how hungry she is.

'I saw a McDonald's on the way here,' she says.

Seema recalls seeing it as well. 'All right we'll go there,' she tells Manpreet.

There is an empty autorickshaw parked on the side of the street. The driver, a short, thickset man, mentions an exorbitant fare for where they want to go. Seema haggles with him. Finally, they arrive at an agreement. Seema motions to Manpreet to get into the autorickshaw. She starts to climb in after her. Then she pauses and turns around to look at where her home had been.

In the last twenty years, she has learnt not to reminisce. No matter where she enters her former life, she finds some aspect of the darkness that swallowed them in 1984 waiting to devour her. Her handsome brother metamorphoses into a burnt corpse. Her parents lose their laughter. Her friends turn their backs on her. Strange people call her all kinds of names and make threatening phone calls... The old house is no exception. Whenever she goes into it, she finds herself at the deep end of the nightmare following Indira Gandhi's assassination and Prem's death.

She had gone to the physical house with Manpreet today, thinking it no longer mattered to her. After all, twenty years had passed. The lump growing in her throat and the tears pushing hard to get out from her eyes tell her how wrong she was.

'Mom.' Manpreet's voice is impatient. She is hungry and wants to get going. Seema swallows, rubbing her eyes. Then she turns around to climb into the autorickshaw. Forcing a smile at Manpreet, she nods to the driver, indicating that he can go.

Acknowledgements

This book would not have been possible without the help and support of several people. First and foremost, my late brother Vijay, who encouraged me through the toughest years and refused to allow me to give up on myself. I would not be a writer if it weren't for him. My agent Preeti Gill believed passionately in the manuscript from day one and worked tirelessly to find a publisher for it. Shalini Krishan, Anurag Basnet and Ravi Singh at Speaking Tiger helped enhance a rough manuscript into the finished book it is today. And finally, my colleagues and employers at Shiv Nadar University who have always supported me in my creative pursuits. I thank you all.

I would also like to salute the countless men and women who suffered in 1984 and who continue to be denied justice to this day. Their indomitable spirit and resilience shines like a beacon despite the darkness that was implanted in their lives more than thirty years ago. They are our true heroes.